Playing for Keeps

Emma Hart

ISBN-13: 978-1490425078
ISBN-10: 1490425071

PLAYING FOR KEEPS is a New Adult Contemporary Romance. This book is intended for mature audiences of 17+. Mature sexual situations, strong language and heavy subject matter are used throughout.

BOOKS BY EMMA HART:

THE GAME SERIES:

NOW AVAILABLE:

The Love Game

Playing for Keeps

The Love Game and Playing for Keeps box set edition

COMING SOON:

The Right Moves – Available March 27th

Worth the Risk – Available May 29th

Acknowledgements

So many people were involved in the making of this book, whether they realized it or not. Some were there at the beginning and many came along the way, but they all had a hand in it.

My critique partner, Rachel Walter, for sitting and listening to my freak outs. You always seem to make sense of things, even when you've said anything at all. Which is ironic because our conversations are usually an awful lot of nonsense. Thank you for all the rants, pow-wows, and hashing it out sessions.

Beta readers – Rachel Walter, Zoe Pope, Alessandra Thomas, Laurelin Paige, Carey Heywood, Heather King, Holly Carter and Christina Pryor. Ignoring that Zoe is British and Holly Australian, thank you for de-Britishing the gang. I'm getting better, but you still catch me.

The best indies I know… Alessandra Thomas, Lauren Blakely, Holly Carter, Karli Perrin, L.M. Augustine and Rachel Brookes. You've all made me smile at some point through writing this book, and your support and friendship means the world. Love always.

WrAHMS: You guys came along the way but you're no less important. You really do keep me sane, and I'm very fond of you and our crazy , 300+ comment chats on things not acceptable to write here.

Bloggers – because I should have mentioned them way, way before now, and I always forgot. This could take a while, but a huge, huge thank you to Zoe Pope at the Book

Lovers, Kristy Garbutt at Book Addict Mumma, Ava Smith at Biblio Belles, Sarah Rostar as Books She Reads, Laura Carter at Bookish Treasures, and Allura LeBlanc at Teacups and Bookends. I'm honoured to have you all read my books, and not only are you all awesome bloggers and total indie fangirls, you're all amazing people, too. And every blogger on my mailing list who helped me promote this book before its release. You have no idea how important you all are to me.

My agent, Daniel Mandel, because whenever I got bogged down I remembered your excitement in our first phone call and it reminded me of why I write. Your support is priceless and I will always value it, and that of Casper Dennis at Abner Stein here in the UK. I definitely lucked out on the agent side!

My partner, Darryl. I'm really running out of things to say for you, so hopefully a thank you for being my formatter will be enough. Maybe I'll dedicate book three to you and go super mushy. Or just buy you a beer. Yeah, let's go for the beer.

My editor at Hachette UK, Anne McNeil. Thank you for all the work you did with me on this new edition of Playing for Keeps. The book is so much stronger now. Thank you for helping me shape it into what it is today. You're fabulous.

Dedication:

This book is for my brother, John, who incidentally will never read it because of the sexy content. He likes to believe my kids were delivered by the stork and that's totally cool.

He's the guy who constantly tells everyone exactly what I'm doing and how successful I've been just because he's proud. I always wanted to be him when I was growing up, but I think I got the better end of the deal.

John, thank you for being the best role model and brother I could have asked for, and for being the support Dad would have been my whole life. I don't tell you often, but I love you, bro.

Chapter One - Megan

"You do realize your mom will ask her one hundred questions about you, right?" I glance up at Braden from my stretched out position on his floor.

"No shit," he mutters. "That's why you need to tell her what to say."

I pause my aimless flicking through my magazine. "Let's think about that for a second."

"Meggy."

"No."

He shuts his closet door and drops to the floor in front of me. His dirty blonde hair flops into his eyes and he levels them on me, pleading with me silently. I shake my head.

"Braden Carter, you chose to take Maddie home for the weekend. You have to deal with – and field – your mom's endless questions."

"Meg," he draws my name out, sounding like a petulant toddler begging for candy.

"It would happen sooner or later." I shrug and sit up, tucking my legs under me. "You might as well get it over with now. Besides," I grin, "I'm sure she'll give the questions a break by telling her childhood stories.

"Fucking hell," Braden grumbles and sighs. "At least I have comfort in the fact you were with me for most of my stupid moments. Hell, you probably caused most of them."

"I so did not!" I pause, and he raises his eyebrows at me. *Actually,* there was that time I ran off with the ladder and left Braden stuck up a tree. We only had the ladder because we had to go to some work thing with our parents, and they didn't want us to be covered in scrapes and grazes. Braden got cocky and thought he could jump – and he could, but not without breaking his arm. We never did get to the work thing … "Okay. At least a third were caused by me. Don't go twisting it, because I will correct her when you come back."

"Yeah, yeah. Whatever you say." He stands and grins. A knock sounds at his door seconds before it's pushed open.

Aston walks in shirtless, his jeans hanging low on his hips. Every inch of his body is exposed, from the curve of his biceps to the dip of his v muscle beneath his pants. My gaze flits over him, taking in his wet hair sticking up, and the small towel slung around his shoulders is almost an afterthought. His gray eyes interrupt my perusal of his body, and he smirks when he realizes.

"I'm starting to wonder if I'll see you anywhere other than a guy's bedroom," he drawls.

"Just because you haven't seen me in yours," I reply, leaning back on my hands. "And I'd imagine that's something you're not used to."

Braden looks to the ceiling and shakes his head, rubbing his hand over his face as if he'd rather be anywhere other than here.

"I don't think you'd fit in in mine." Aston leans

against the doorframe. "It's not up to the standards a pretty little rich girl is used to."

"I can't say fitting in with your bedroom is on my to-do list." Even if the person is … "And pretty little rich girl I may be, but I'm not a snob."

Aston snorts. "So if a guy from, say, a shit-riddled and utterly fucked up background chatted you up, you wouldn't run ten miles in the other direction?"

I stand, staring at him. "Just because someone's past and upbringing is fucked up doesn't mean the person is, Aston. The way someone was brought up doesn't define them as a person. Whatever perception you have of me, however stuck up you think I am – my upbringing doesn't define the person I am now. I'm not as shallow as you'd like to think I am."

He tilts his head to the side for a moment before his lips twitch up at one side. It's a cocky, smug grin that tells me I walked right into his trap.

"Oh, it's easy," he says through his smile. "So, so easy. You're a little ticking time bomb aren't you, Megan?"

"Any reason you're here?" Braden interjects before I can respond.

"Yeah. I need that English book." Aston looks around.

"Which one? I've got more fucking English books than I have classes."

"Shit, man, I dunno." Aston shrugs. "The one from last class."

I roll my eyes and perch on the edge of Braden's

bed. "The Shakespeare one."

Both of them look at me blankly, Braden more so. Aston at least looks like he knows who Shakespeare is.

"You know, Bray. The guy who lived 'years ago and can't fuckin' talk properly'." I give Braden a pointed look, and his face breaks into a big grin.

"Oh, that guy. Yeah. I pretty much reworded Maddie's work." Braden turns to his desk and grabs the textbook. He shoves it in Aston's direction.

"Cheers, dude." Aston looks at me and winks, and I try not to roll my eyes again.

He's so damn infuriating. He really does wind me up just 'cause he knows it's easy, and he's starting to learn that referring to me as "a little rich girl" is the easiest way to rile me. It's not my fault I was born into an upper middle class family – Braden was too, and he doesn't get the rich boy treatment.

Oh, that's right. He doesn't get it because eighty percent of the guys in this house are from the same background.

I reach down, grab my magazine from the floor and roll it up. I swing it in Braden's direction, smacking his back with it.

"Ouch! What the fuck was that for?" He frowns at me.

"Thanks for backing me up, dickhead."

"Hey – I shut him up."

I scoff. "Only because you were getting annoyed that I and his bedroom were put in the same sentence."

"At least I shut him up. Now you can tell Maddie

what to say to my mom."

Oh, I'll tell her what to say alright.

I sigh, looking into his wide, pleading eyes, and shrug. "Fine, I'll tell her what to say."

~

"I think you were playing your own game all along." Lila twirls a bit of hair around her finger.

My lips quirk behind the safety of my book, and I glance at her over the top of it. "I have no idea what you're talking about."

"You're a terrible liar, Megs. You know exactly what I'm talking about."

"If I knew I wouldn't have asked."

She reaches over and tugs my book down, catching my smile before I can hide it again.

"See!" she exclaims. "You do know."

"Okay, okay. So what if I was? It all worked out in the end, didn't it?"

"But it nearly didn't. Maddie ran back to Brooklyn, or did you forget that?"

"No," I reply slowly. "I didn't forget that. She came back and they kicked each other's asses."

She purses her lips. "You weren't worried at all were you?"

I shake my head. "Not really. I know that makes me sound horrible, like I don't care, but I knew they'd sort it out. You can't tell me you believed her when she said she wasn't in love with him?"

"Well no . . ."

"Precisely. She fell for him as hard as he fell for her, Lila."

"Then why Brooklyn? I just don't get it. We all know they were doing the same thing."

"You weren't here when Braden found out." I chew on my bottom lip. That was the worst moment – none of us ever thought he'd turn up at her dorm room, least of all me. It was a bad call on my part, and despite my best efforts to get rid of the poster there was no way to do it quietly. "He was mad. So, so damn mad. I sat there and watched his heart break, Li, and I felt so shit. Hell, I watched both their hearts break. What did it for Maddie was Braden went crazy over what she was doing, then she found out he was doing the exact same thing. She was embarrassed over the whole thing and angry over how he'd acted. But most of all she was heartbroken over it – that moment shattered every belief she had that he'd fallen in love with her. The only thing she could do was run."

"Huh. And she told you that?"

"No, but you don't have to be cupid to figure it out."

"How did you figure it out?"

I shrug a shoulder. "It happens when your favorite aunt is qualified in three areas of psychology."

Her mouth drops open. "Three?"

"I know, I know. I come from a family of overachievers. I think I'm somewhat of a disappointment with my little English major and book writing ambition."

"At least you're doing what you love. And, for the record, you'd be a terrible cupid." She giggles.

"Well, thanks." I throw my pillow at her, smiling. "But like I said, it's all okay now, isn't it?"

"I have to admit, I never thought I'd see the day Braden Carter took a girl home." Lila hugs my pillow to her chest.

"You and I both." I smirk.

I never truly thought I'd see the day he'd be as in love as he is. Braden and Maddie have the magical kind of love every little girl dreams of – at least I did. I spent hours upon hours dreaming of the guy that would give me butterflies and sweep me so high off my feet I'd never go back down. My dreams were only fueled by Mom's extensive library in her home office. I can't count the times I used to sneak books out to read about the kind of love my best friends are experiencing now.

"Whatcha readin'?" Nanna peered over my shoulder.

I jumped, snapping the book shut. "Nothing."

"Why you readin' it then?"

"Dunno."

She leaned over the back of the sofa and snatched the book out of my hands. My eyes widened as she took in the book. "Huckleberry Finn? You're hiding for this?"

"Um, yeah." I swallowed.

Nanna opened the book. Her eyes flicked across a page before she closed it again and pulled off the dust jacket. "Megan Harper. You sneaky devil."

I smiled warily.

"Does your mother know you've stolen her copy of Pride and Prejudice when you should be reading Huck Finn?"

"No. Please don't tell her, Nanna! Huck Finn isn't terrible, but I don't want to read it. I'd much rather read about Lizzy and Darcy."

She didn't respond.

"Please, Nanna."

"I won't say a word, girl. Between you and me, Huck Finn isn't nearly as exciting as Mr. Darcy. Just don't tell your mother I approve of your stealing her romance novels."

"I won't."

Nanna gestured to the book. "Has he kissed her yet?"

I nodded happily. "It's my favorite part."

"Mine too." She winked.

Our dorm door opens, snapping me out of my inner musings, and Maddie comes bursting in in an explosion of fiery hair.

"You have to make me ill or something. Or pretend I am. Or – oh! Cover me in face paint," she babbles, slamming the door and pressing her back against it.

"Eh? Face paint?" I frown.

"Yep. I'm allergic." She gestures to her face. "Makes my face go all puffy and spotty and stuff."

"Aside from the fact face paint isn't something I keep

under my bed," Lila comments. "Why on Earth do you want to be ill?"

Maddie slumps down the door, hugging her knees to her chest. "I've never ... You know. Done the meeting the parents thing before."

"Ohhh," Lila and I say in unison.

"His parents aren't bad at all." I look at her. "Honestly, they're some of the nicest people I've ever met."

"He's your best friend. You have to say that," she groans.

"Well, he is, but I don't. Really, Mads. You don't have to be worried about anything."

"What if they ask me a hundred questions?"

"His dad won't. His mom will, though – but not about you. About Braden."

"And what do I say?"

"The truth." I grin. "Aha! I win!"

Maddie and Lila both look toward me, their eyebrows raised.

"I told Braden I'd tell Maddie what to say to his mom, and I'm saying to tell the truth."

"Smart move," Lila acknowledges.

"I guess he didn't tell you to convince me to lie?" Maddie sits up and smiles.

"Of course he didn't. He naturally assumes I will do that, and more fool him." I grin. "When are you going?"

"After English. We have it last tomorrow, don't we?"

I nod, and Lila frowns. "I thought you were going

Saturday morning. Something about Braden not wanting to leave Megs for two nights to party in a house full of horny frat boys."

I drop my head back. "For fuck sake," I mutter to the ceiling.

"Oh, that was the first plan," Maddie explains. "I told him he was being damn ridiculous, and Megan was more than capable of looking after herself in a house full of animals."

My head moves forward, and I smile gratefully at her. "See." I glance Lila's way. "This is another reason I knew they'd be perfect for each other. She kicks his ass, and I get a break from his adorable protective act."

"Adorably annoying," Maddie corrects me. "It drives me mad, so I have no idea how you put up with it."

"It's normal for me. He's always done it, so it doesn't really bother me anymore. It's a bit like white noise now. Besides, I already begged his mom to give him a baby sister when I was thirteen, and she refused."

"Wow, was he really that bad?" Lila snickers.

"You really want to know?" I glance between them, and they nod. "Okay, we were six and it was fall. We'd spent all weekend collecting conkers for school on Monday, and I had the perfect one. Braden always won against me, but I'd won our practice battle on the way to school with it. There was this boy who had a kiddie crush on me – Adam Land. I challenged him to a conker fight and won. He hated being beaten by a girl, so threw another one at my head. Braden jumped on him and bit him."

"He bit him?!" Maddie shrieks, and Lila laughs.

I put my hand to my mouth and giggle silently as I nod. "He bit him so hard he drew blood. His mom went crazy when the principal called her."

"That's brilliant. I wish my brother would have done that. He would have laughed," Lila muses.

"Okay, now I'm really glad I talked him into going tomorrow no matter how worried I am about it." Maddie tries to muffle her giggles.

"Does this mean I get to see a different side of Megan?" Lila asks, a glint in her eyes.

"Hey, it doesn't mean I'm gonna grab some guy by his collar and drag him to bed just because Braden isn't here." I drop my eyes to the floor. "Maybe."

Besides, I flit through a perpetual state of love-hate where the guy I want to take to bed is concerned. I live the Elizabeth and Mr. Darcy kind of love in *Pride and Prejudice*. Luckily enough everyone else only sees the hate.

The fact crazy little butterflies fire up in my stomach whenever Aston Banks walks into a room is my secret. And I don't intend to share it anytime soon.

Chapter Two - Aston

Her blue eyes are focused on the words on the page in front of her like they always are. I've never known anyone to spend as much time with their nose between the pages of a book as Megan does. Everywhere she goes she has one – in her bag, in her lap, next to her.

No one else notices. And no one else notices the fact I do.

Her brow furrows, and she sucks her bottom lip into her mouth as she sweeps her long blonde hair from her face. She gathers it at the back of her head and snaps a band from her wrist, tying it up and exposing the sleek curve of her neck and the skin there. I spin my pen between my fingers and glance at my own book.

Off limits. That's what Megan Harper is.

I knew the first time I saw her I could never have her. The way she holds herself and the sarcastic yet polite comments – she has endless amounts of "screams rich girl", a class I never have and never will be in. It's engrained in her to treat everyone with respect no matter what you think of them. I'm certain she could face a serial killer and have at least one nice comment for him.

She does for everyone.

Everyone is treated the same way, and every sarcastic, almost bitchy comment is followed by a softer one. Every frown or fleeting dirty look is followed by an apologetic smile and every slap is a playful one. Everyone is equal until they prove her otherwise.

Except me.

I'm the exception to her rule. And I fucking love it. I bring it on myself, but I can't help getting under her skin and shaking her up. It's addictive, sparking a fire in me I can't put out once I've started. She bites so easily and her voice snaps a reply to me sometimes before I can even finish what I'm saying.

It makes it easier to keep away from her. Makes it easier to take a random girl I don't give a shit about to my room every weekend and fuck her instead. If Megan showed even one ounce of interest in me for something other than a battle of words, I'd be next to her like a damn gunshot.

I'd have her in my bed and underneath me quicker than a fucking bullet.

"What's the matter? Bored of looking at your usual tarts?"

I blink. Her face is turned toward me, her large, bright eyes questioning, and I smirk.

"Depends if you include yourself in that statement."

"I don't exactly have a high opinion of myself, Aston, but I don't think quite that badly of myself either." She bites the end of her pen. "The last thing I'd want is to be one of your tarts."

Ouch.

"That's a shame." I lean in closer. "I think you'd fit in perfectly."

"Really?" She smiles insincerely. "'Cause I'm afraid I don't quite make the cut. For one, my panties tend to still be on by the end of the night."

"It could be arranged for it to be otherwise."

"The only way they'll be coming off is if I take them off myself."

I grin. She's getting the tell-tale flush to her cheeks, and her eyes are shining a little more like they always do when she's annoyed. Shit, I've been on the receiving end of this look enough times.

"Hey." I lean back, resting my foot on top of my other knee. "Whatever floats your boat, babe. I'm not against a little striptease."

Megan runs her tongue across the top of her teeth and stares me down. "Then go and look in your goddamn mirror, 'cause you aren't getting one from me."

I can't help the upturn of my lips just like I can't help the images in my head. Her jeans are tight enough, I don't need to imagine the curve of her ass, but I do imagine it minus the jeans and her bent over, pulling her underwear down.

Blood rushes down my body and I shift. Jesus - a hard on in English isn't what I need.

"Another shame." I drop my hands to my lap. Fucking thing has a mind of its own. "You have just enough ass to get it right."

"So do you, but I don't see you standing in front of my table and ripping your clothes off to a cheesy tune." She barely bats an eyelid, taking her eyes from mine and going back to her word. "And thank God I don't."

"Braden goes tonight," I say, changing the subject completely.

"I know."

"Are you coming over?"

Her eyes scoot from the page to meet mine. "Why?"

"Because I was wondering if I could get that striptease," I reply sarcastically. "Fucking hell, Megan. I was just asking."

She rolls her eyes – something I'm sure she has reserved for when she talks to me. "Alright! Yes, I am. I'm coming over with Lila and Kay."

"Your little sidekicks." I smirk.

"Says you," she mutters.

I'll ignore that. "So you'll be at a party without Braden. How will you cope?"

"Fuck you, Aston."

"Sore spot, huh?"

She spins in her chair and fully levels her gaze on me. Sparks fire in the blue, and I know I've really pissed her off this time.

Just as well I like it when she's mad at me.

"I'm not a china doll, much to everyone's disappointment," she snaps. "I don't need Braden to hold my hand when I'm at a party, thank you very much. I'm more than capable of keeping away horny assholes. I'm not sure where you've gotten your perceptions of me from, but they're so wrong it's unreal."

She slams her books shut as everyone gets up. She

storms past me, then pauses a second and looks back at me over her shoulder. Her lips part, but she shakes her head, turning around and walking away instead.

My perceptions of you are just fine, I want to say as I watch her leave. I just don't say what I really think, because that would be counter-productive to keeping away from the one girl I really want.

~

Same shit, different night.

The house is full of people, some from Berkeley and some not. I'm getting to the point where I don't even fucking know. The only reason I'm in this damn frat house is because Gramps was and it was what he wanted. Hell, the man has done enough for me. The least I could do was apply and get in here for him.

Girls flutter their eyelashes, flick their hair, and skim their eyes through the people to find a guy to take home. The guys do their version of it; standing against the bar, walls, in doorways, drinking beer and picking out a girl to take wherever the fuck they want to. And I'm doing it too.

Same as always. Friday and Saturday nights equal meaningless sex. Focusing on that, the meaningless fuck, means I can't focus on the shit that means something. And it's so easy.

Pick a girl. Hand her a drink. Tell her she's pretty. Take her upstairs. Fuck her. Make sure she's gone by morning.

I'm not the only one that keeps to that. Braden used to, and half the guys in this house do as well. The girls know exactly what they're getting themselves into, at least with me – they know I want nothing more than a couple hours.

I don't even want to know their damn name.

I bring my beer bottle to my lips and glance at a tall, dark haired girl walking past. Her eyes skirt down to me and her lips curl. She's not perfect, but she'd do ... If I wasn't so aware of a pair of eyes on me.

I fight the impulse to meet the gaze across the room but lose. I let my eyes jump from the girl to Megan's. She's sitting at the bar, her body facing it, the angle almost begging me to take note of the way her dress hugs her body. I trace my eyes over it, and I love the fact she's got more curves than most of the girls here. She's not the skinniest girl but she's confident in her body and it shows.

Confidence is pretty hot on any girl, but on Megan it's just downright sexy.

I smirk at her, my lips moving slowly, and raise an eyebrow. Her foot taps as she holds my gaze, neither of us willing to look away, and something shifts between us. She swallows and runs her fingers through her hair, her eyelids drooping. The movement is so slight I only notice because I'm looking for it. Because I'm looking for any little thing that will show me the shift is attraction.

And it is.

She purses her lips around the straw in her glass and questions me with her eyes. This is different – it isn't us trying to piss each other off. It isn't us throwing sarcastic comments at each other. It's something new.

Something raw.

Something dangerous.

Something that could fuck me up.

The smirk drops from my face, and she looks away. She swirls the ice cubes round the bottom of her empty glass and her shoulders relax slightly. I spin the beer bottle between my fingers.

I know the risks. I know if I go over there the sex tonight won't be meaningless. It won't be a casual fuck where it doesn't matter in the morning. It'll be giving in to the one weakness I have.

But fuck. I want to.

Chapter Three - Megan

I want to be the girl going upstairs with him instead of the one watching him go.

He drives me crazy in the worst kind of way. Every comment, every smirk, every cocky raise of his eyebrows. Each thing affects me, especially the way he clearly doesn't know me even though he thinks he does. He's so wrong about me in every way, and it pisses me off so badly, yet I don't think I could say no if he walked up to me right now and invited me to his room.

The one not fit for a little rich girl like me.

The one I'd probably feel totally at home with.

But I don't know if one night would be enough. When you want someone so badly you have to work to hide it, just one night of letting go of that restraint wouldn't be enough. If he came up to me now and I let go, I don't think I'd be able to hold on again. I don't think I'd be able to leave it at one night of casual sex.

Hell. I don't know if sex with him would be casual.

I know one night can't hurt, but I also know it can't do any good.

"Sex doesn't make love, Megan. If you want to give physically, that's up to you, but don't give it all up emotionally just because a guy has a few smooth lines or is good looking. Real sex is the whole package."

And Mom's words remind me I want the whole package now.

"I don't think I've ever seen you alone," Aston's voice crawls over me smoothly, making the hairs on the back of my neck stand up, and he sits on the stool next to me.

"It doesn't happen often." I turn my face slowly, finding his gray eyes for the umpteenth time today. "I could say the same to you."

"It doesn't happen often," he parrots, a half-smile teasing his lips.

"So why are you here with me and not in a dark corner with your usual company?"

"Ouch, Megan. Is that bitterness in your voice?" His knees brush mine. "Don't tell me you're jealous."

"Disgust," I mutter, looking away from him so he doesn't catch the lie. "Don't confuse it with bitterness or jealousy."

"You know something?" He leans in closer, his breath fluttering my hair as he places his mouth close to my ear. "I think you're fooling yourself. Ten minutes, Megan."

He gets up and disappears, leaving me shaking my head after him. I need to shake my head – I need to do something to hide the temptation running through my body.

Kyle wordlessly removes my glass and pours me another drinks. "You're quiet tonight." He leans against the bar opposite me.

"It has been known to happen." I smile.

"Odd without Mads and Braden, huh?"

I shrug a shoulder. "A bit, I guess. At least all their shit is sorted out now. We can all get on with our lives."

Kyle snorts. "Right. Braden took every guy in this house down with him when she went to Brooklyn. It was like living with a woman with fucking PMS, and shit, I moved away from home to escape that. My sister is a demon then."

"You should try being around guys that don't get laid enough," I comment dryly, sipping my drink. "They beat girls with PMS hands down."

"I don't doubt it." He smirks. "Just so happens there's none of those around here."

"Huh. You're probably right."

"You look like you need to get laid though."

"And here I was thinking you were a nice guy. You had to go and blow it by saying that, didn't you?" I sigh playfully. "You all are the same."

"Hey, I'm just saying." He leans forward and grins. "I bet you wouldn't be short of offers since the caveman isn't here."

I bite the inside of my cheek, fighting my smile. "The caveman thing is really sticking, huh?"

"You have no idea." Kyle's eyes twinkle.

Why can't I want Kyle instead? He's a damn nice guy, and he's not exactly bad looking without his unruly dark hair and hazel eyes. He's leanly built, his muscles not showy but clear to see. He'd be such a great distraction – if

I wasn't already so distracted by Aston.

I finish the rest of my drink and push the glass toward him. "Do me a favor? Tell Lila I'll see her tomorrow sometime. I'm heading back to the dorm."

"Got it." He nods and turns away.

I glance around the room and scoot out of it. This is a risk. A big risk, but I don't care.

Aston's words were full of promises when he sat next to me on the stool, and his eyes were full of mysteries I want to unravel between his sheets. Paranoia attaches itself to me as I push my way through the living room and up the stairs. I run my fingers through my hair as if I'm just heading to the bathroom and glance around on the landing. My fingers grasp the bottom of my dress and tug it down as I climb the final staircase to his room.

Someone grabs my arm and spins me into the wall. Their mouth covers mine, swallowing my shriek, and their swift movements thwart my attempt at kneeing them in the balls.

"You're not being attacked," Aston mutters lowly against my mouth. "Unless you want it."

I open my eyes to his in the dim light of the hallway. "You're a pig, you know that?"

"Yet you're here."

"Apparently." I drop my eyes.

He cups the side of my head, threading his fingers through my hair, and tugs my face upward. His lips touch mine again, soft but forceful, and I slide my hands up his arms to grip his collar. I hold his face against mine, parting my lips for his probing mouth, and push my body into his. He flicks his tongue against mine, before biting on my bottom lip and sweeping it across it. Tremors fall down my spine, and he reaches around to slot his key into the door, breaking the kiss.

He shoves it open, his hands trailing down my back, and I let him pull me into his room. He slams the door at the same time he yanks my body against his, his breath fanning across my lips. My eyes drop to his mouth and close as he dips his head to kiss me again. This time it's firmer, more needing, and my fingers creep below his polo shirt and onto his hot skin. I spread my fingers out, my thumbs brushing the solid muscle on his stomach, and he releases me to pull his shirt over his head.

I run my bottom lip between my teeth and run my eyes down his torso. He's perfect, beautifully so. His skins stretches over each pack of muscle, the shadows in the indents between them like a light engraving on his skin.

I step forward and touch my mouth to his chest, and he cups the back of my head. He kisses my earlobe, running his lips down my neck, and my trembling hands reach up between us.

What am I doing?

"Megan?"

I open my mouth to speak but no words come out. Instead I swallow, stepping back. His hands fall away from me and hang limply at his sides.

"I …" I swallow again, trying to control the crazy buzzing in the back of my mind. "This … This can't happen."

Can't happen? What am I doing now?

"Can't happen?" He looks like he's at a complete loose end, unable to work out what I'm saying. Hell, I just followed him up here and now I'm refusing. I don't get it myself.

"Yep." I back toward the door, pushing my hair from my face, and tug my dress down a little. "This can't happen. At all."

My hand finds the handle and opens the door. And I walk away, leaving him staring after me.

~

No one knows.

I remind myself of this as I stare at Lila's sleeping body. I keep expecting her to wake up and yell at me for being so dumb. But no one knows – not that it's stopping the intense feelings of near-peace and guilt warring inside me.

The old age cliché. Your head vs. your heart. My head is telling what I already know – I'm a terrible person. I betrayed my best friend by kissing his best friend when I know it's the last thing he wanted me to do … But my heart tells me differently, what I should know. It's telling me I'm not a terrible person. For once I went after what I wanted without thinking of the consequences.

It doesn't make me reckless and unfeeling. So unfeeling is probably an exaggeration, but reckless? Yes. It was reckless, and probably a little selfish.

Then again, you don't get anywhere in life without pissing off a few people.

Was last night a mistake? I did the one thing I said I wouldn't do, the one thing I promised myself I wouldn't fucking do. Don't get involved with your best friend's best friend – it's simple. Something so simple that became incredibly complicated the second I looked into Aston's misty gray eyes the first day of college. I always knew there'd be something between us, I just didn't know if it would amount to anything.

And here we are.

After all my attempts, all my fighting to keep away from him, I've still somehow ended up falling for his cocky smile and man-whore ways. Not that I love the man-whore ways – I want to set fire to the fake hair, fake nails, and fake eyelashes of every girl that sleeps with him. That's what they are, and he knows it. Fake.

Jesus Christ, Megan, it was a freaking kiss. One little kiss. Not a goddamn proposal.

But … Maddie said Braden would never fall in love but she was wrong. He did, but Braden and Aston are in different leagues. Braden's heart was never truly in the sleeping around, he just did it because he could. Something to pass the time – I know that as clearly as I know Aston likes the sleeping around and never-ending attention he gets from girls.

How has one little kiss ended in me dissecting his behavior? A kiss!

I don't have any expectations for an "us". I have wants but no expectations. I may be a hopeless romantic happy to get lost between the pages of a hot and steamy novel or a sigh-with-sweetness one, but I'm not naïve enough to believe that those kinds of things happen all the time. Some people will get that kind of love that makes guys wonder and girls swoon, but not everyone.

Love is a fickle thing. Just because you have a person out there that compliments you, that calms your storm and feeds your fire, it doesn't mean you'll always have them. You might never meet them. You might meet them – but it just might not be the right time for you.

I'm nineteen. I know love and lust. I know the difference – and I know that for some strange reason, Aston is my storm calmer, my fire feeder. I also know it isn't the right time for us. It might never be.

Though after the way he held me to him and kissed me last night, I'm not so sure I'm okay with that anymore.

Chapter Four - Aston

I'm fucked. And it's all my own fault.

I had to do it, didn't I? I had to go over to her and say what I did. I didn't expect her to do it – I never thought she'd actually come upstairs, but she did. And shit; it felt so wrong but so right at the same time.

She's so dangerous. She's the one in this whole damn college, hell, in the whole damn state, that could strip away my devil-may-care attitude and put me on my sorry ass. She's the only girl that could make me feel again. She could take everything I've tried for so long to stick back together and shatter it into more pieces than it was in in the first place.

I should have stayed the fuck away from her, but I didn't. And now I know the sweet taste of her mouth as she kissed me. I know the softness of her lips as they moved across mine, and I know the feel of her hands gripping my hair.

I also know what it's like to be so close but so far away. 'Cause damn it all to hell, she had to stop and walk away, didn't she? She had to fucking go and leave me there, as hard as a rock, staring after her like a lost little sheep.

Shit. Even though it was just a kiss, it's gonna take nothing short of a goddamn miracle to get me to stay away from her now.

I grab my cell from the side and scroll to her name.

I'm pretty sure I showed Old Maid up last night. Bet the old girl can't kiss the way I can. I press send, remembering the conversation in Vegas, and my lips curve.

Learn some tricks from the big boys in Vegas, did you? She retorts. I'd bet anything she's smiling that smile that lights up her whole face. The smile that makes her looks so damn beautiful she'd put every girl in the country to shame.

You tell me, babe. I grin wider.

I roll over in bed and hit the empty side – the empty side she lay on last night before she left while I was sleeping. My eyes find the calendar on the bedside table, and I shove it off the top to avoid looking at the date. But I know it.

I always know it. It's impossible to ignore – it creeps up on me silently then hits me with a big fucking bang. It's always the hardest this time of year. This week, the one that shaped my life, is the one I love and hate. It changed me for the better but forever destroyed my Gramps.

One person's blessing is another person's curse.

I jump out of bed, get dressed, and grab my car keys. It's earlier than usual and Gramps will probably whack me with his stick for turning up before lunch, but I have no desire to sit here in my room and wallow in my own bullshit self-pity.

I slip out of the front door before anyone stops me and climb into my car, quickly pulling away from the large house. It can become stifling all too quickly, and it's easy to get buried under the weight of your own feelings. It's not too far to Gramps' house, his insistence on moving us away from San Francisco but not out of Northern California the reason I'm at college in Berkeley and not there. San Francisco holds too many memories. Too much shit to ever go back to.

I pull up outside his house, the sun crawling over the front yard an indication I'll spend my day working in his back yard doing what he can't. The rich smell of smoke wafting from his cigar hits me as soon as I open the door, and my face wrinkles up like it does every Sunday.

I hate it, but it's safe – and there's comfort in safety.

"I wish you'd stop smokin' those damn things, Gramps."

His low, raspy chuckle reaches me through the house. "You say that e'ry week, boy, and I'll keep on saying the same thing back – I wish you'd stop goin' on about me smoking these 'damn things'."

I grin and make my way into the front room, letting the front door swing shut behind me. The old, wrinkled man I call my Gramps is sitting in his usual spot in front of the window. The floral chair is as old and weathered as he is, but there's definitely more life left in Gramps than in his ratty chair.

"I know. It's worth the shot, though, right?" I shrug, dropping onto the sofa across from him.

He smiles as he turns his face toward me, his dark gray eyes crinkling a little in the corners. "If you say so, boy. What are you doin' here early, bugging me?"

I look out of the window. "Got nothin' better to do on a Sunday."

He chuckles. "Never know, do I? Probably did what you had to do last night."

"Gramps. Someone your age shouldn't be making comments like that."

"Why? Because I'm wrinkled? Find me a nice bit of stuff on a Friday at the Bingo, and I'll put you to shame. Ha!" He puffs one last time on his cigar and stubs it out in the ashtray on the table next to him.

"So many things wrong with that damn sentence." I shake my head.

"So, who'd you annoy this time?"

"Who says I annoyed someone?"

"You're here at half ten in the mornin', boy! Something is up. You never get your sorry ass out of bed earlier than twelve on a Sunday."

"I didn't annoy anyone. Besides, I knew you'd want my 'sorry ass' in your yard today."

Gramps' knowing gray eyes settle on me. He taps his fingers on the arm on his chair, each knock of his fingers grating on me. Time stretches as he searches my face, coming to his conclusion. I swallow and shake my head.

"I know what you're gonna say, and you're wrong," I say firmly.

He starts softly. "You've never spoken about her."

"I don't want to speak about her. I have *nothing* to say about her."

"I think you do. I think you just pretend you don't."

I shake my head and look away. "And I think you're shittin' me, Gramps. I get it, alright? You miss her and you wanna talk about her, but I don't. I can't relate to the Mom you knew. She was never, and I mean *never,* that person to me."

"You can't live in hate forever, boy."

"It's not hate, Gramps. It's pity, pure and simple. I pity her and I pity the life she forced me to lead until she died – until you took me in."

"For all your schoolin', for everything I taught you, you never learned to forgive and forget?" he says in a softer voice, his tone coaxing my eyes back to his.

"Forgiving and forgetting are two very different things, Gramps. You can forgive, you can forget, but rarely are they done together. I can't forget my childhood and I can't erase the scars. I can't change the things it's taught me or burn those images or memories from my mind. They mean I'll never forget, and because I can't forget, I can't forgive. It's that simple."

His gray eyes darken slightly with disappointment and sadness. The usual pang of guilt hits me – guilt for hating the person he loves. Guilt for relief in his despair.

"Gramps-"

"No." He drags his gaze back to the window, his focus on the yard outside. "I understand. I just wish I understood you, boy."

"Nothin' to understand," I reply. "I'm just getting on with it, Gramps. I can't let myself live in the crap of my past. Not now, not ever."

"There's some weedin' that needs doing in the far corner, by my vegetable garden. When that's done, I need some holes diggin' for some bushes I'm getting this week."

I take the subject change – and the escape. Both of us, we're always running away from what we want to say. What we need to say.

"Bushes?"

"For your Nan. Hydrangea. Always Hydrangea," he mutters to himself. "For devotion and understanding. We all need a little of that."

I nod although he's not looking at me. His way of remembering her. I wonder if he's glad that Nan never saw what happened to her only daughter. I wonder if he's glad that for all the pain she suffered, she never had to watch her baby destroy herself and die.

I wonder what she would think of me now, if she'd look at me and be happy I'm her grandson, or find comfort in my plans for the future. I wonder what she'd say about the way I cope and how I act.

I grab the trowel from the shed, crouching by the vegetable garden, and the truth smacks me full in the face.

Nan would probably be disgusted by me.

God knows there isn't much to be fucking proud of.

Chapter Five - Megan

My eyes scan the room, and I sigh in relief when I see I've beaten both Aston and Braden to class. Every part of me wishes it was a day where we didn't share a class, but it just doesn't work that way. This is real life, and as my Nanna always says, real life likes to kick you when you're down.

I sit down at my desk and remember who sits with me. Shit. I drop my head, resting it on the table.

"Crap," I mutter.

The chair next to me squeaks. "If you're trying to hide, babe, then you're doing a shit job. I can see you." Aston's words curve around me, wrapping me in a smooth caress, and my throat goes dry.

"Why would I be hiding?" I sit up and forward, determined not to meet his eyes.

He shrugs a shoulder carelessly, grabbing his pen and twirling it between his fingers. God – I hate it when he does that. I catch his every movement from the corner of my eye. His eyes are burning in the side of my head, begging me to turn, begging to look at him.

"Because you want me so badly you can't even look at me," he says in a dramatic tone, arrogance weaving through each word.

My back straightens. "Clearly someone's been feeding your damn ego again. I remember being the one who walked away – and I don't remember ever telling you I want you."

He leans forward and his bicep brushes mine, the heat from the fleeting touch sinking through the sleeve of my sweater. "Is that so?" he asks, his voice low and barely perceptible.

I fight the urge to drop my eyes to the desk. "Damn right it is."

He trails his fingertip down the back of my arm, the tickling feeling leaving me tingling and fighting a shiver. "I think you're wrong," he whispers. "You might have walked away, Megan Harper, but you were also the one that walked toward me." His eyes flick to my lips. "And it was a damn nice walk, don't you think?"

My head snaps round, leaving our faces inches apart. His lips are curled in a slightly smug smile, and I curse myself for that being the first place my eyes fell. I drag them away from his mouth and across the sharp planes of his face until they meet his smoky eyes.

And I remember why I didn't want to look at him. His eyes have the power to entrance me, to hold me captive in his gaze, and they are. The silvery hint at the edge of his irises is pulling me in and trapping my eyes in a silent battle with his. Like this, when I'm unable to focus on anything but the swirling mass of gray in front of me, I remember why nothing could have stopped me following him and kissing him on Saturday night.

"Is he being an asshole again?"

My eyes shift from gray to blue as Braden's voice cuts

through the fog Aston put me in. "That's a stupid question, Bray. He's always an asshole."

Braden grins and jabs Aston in the arm. "Get your slimy mitts away from her, dude. I told you in Vegas, she's got more fucking class than your usual lot."

"I know that," Aston replies, moving his gaze across my face.

I tear my eyes away, trying not to laugh at the irony of Braden's statement. I might have more class than his usual weekenders, but that doesn't mean I'm not one of them. I just won't go and beg for more.

"Coffee?" Maddie mouths across the room, catching my eye. I nod – I want to know how the weekend went for them. Braden's mom can be a little … eccentric sometimes.

"I take it he doesn't know?" Aston nudges my foot with his.

I jolt, glancing back to him as Braden sits next to Maddie. "Um, no. Aside from the fact that's the first time I've seen him, I can't just drop it into a conversation, can I? That would be fun."

"I guess not." He rubs his thumb over his mouth. "Besides–"

"Let me guess," I deadpan. "Your face is too good to be messed up by the fist that would inevitably meet it?"

He pauses for a second and smirks. "I wasn't gonna say that, but I'm glad you think so."

"You know, Aston, Braden isn't the only one capable of messing up your pretty face."

"I like a girl feisty."

"And you also like to discard them after a quick and meaningless fuck, never mind a mere kiss against a wall, so it doesn't really matter, does it?" I raise an eyebrow, feeling the pang of my own harsh words.

He stops, and I turn away. My own words have stung me more than I thought they could. No matter how many times I tell myself I don't care, I do. I care more than I want to. No one wants to be tossed aside like a ragdoll by the person they want to care.

"I never said you were a mere kiss, Megs, neither would be a quick and meaningless fuck. Don't put words in my fucking mouth," he whispers as the lesson starts. He leans forward, still twirling his pen between his fingers. "I'm many things and not all of them are good, but I'm not a liar. I'd be lying if I said that kiss was nothing."

A lump rises in my throat, full of hope and wanting ... And reality. It's full of emotions that have no place in this conversation. I swallow the words forming in my mouth, the ones full of truth that have no place in a time of doubt, and I swallow the question I don't want to hear the answer to.

All I want to do right now is ignore him and focus on class, but it's nearly impossible. I can feel every inch of him beside me, I can see each movement of his body and I can sense every flicker of his eyes to me.

Aston stretches his leg out under the table and knocks his foot into mine. I tuck my feet under my chair and sweep my hair to one side so it falls into a curtain between us. I need something to block us – I'm too aware of him and the way he makes me feel.

A tug on my hair pulls me from my forced state of concentration, and my neck almost snaps with the force of my head turning.

"What?" I hiss.

"Are you avoiding me?"

"I'm sitting right next to you. How the hell can I be avoiding you?"

"Well would you be sitting here if you didn't have to?"

"No. But the same applies to every time I have to sit next to you, so today isn't anything special."

He sits back, his face deathly serious. "You think I'm a total jackass."

"Do you want a gold star? I thought it was obvious." The lessons ends, and I shove all my things in my bag. I stand and hoist it over my shoulder when he grabs my arm.

"Just remember, Megan," he whispers from behind me, "who came to who on Saturday night. And I bet you'd do it again in a heartbeat."

Fuck. Smartass little dick.

I watch him go and I hate that he's right. He might have put his cards on the table, but I'm the one that collected them and shuffled them. That stupid, stupid kiss was my own doing, and we both know it.

We both know I can pretend to hate him. We also both know it's a big bag of bullshit.

"Ready to go?" Maddie holds the door open, and I

glare at Aston's retreating back.

"As long as we don't run into anymore assholes while we're there, then let's go," I mumble.

"What did he do?" she asks with a hint of laughter.

"He's just being Aston." I shrug. "You know – his usual Gods-gift-to-women self."

"Mmph. Was he like that all weekend?"

"I have no idea. I barely saw him," I lie and inwardly flinch. Damn. I hate lying, yet here I am.

"Probably just as well," she muses, smoothing her hair back from her face. "Braden nearly combusted this weekend with the thought he'd left you here in Berkeley around his, and I quote, 'will fuck anything with a pulse' friend."

I force a laugh. "You'd think Braden has no faith in my ability to stay away from someone like that."

And rightly so.

Maddie shrugs. "You know what he's like. Of course his mom heard his frequent use of vulgar words and handed him his ass on a silver platter."

I laugh loudly and this time it's real. "Oh, man. I wish I could have seen that!"

"It was hilarious." She giggles. "She kept asking me if he's that vile at college."

"What did you say?" I peruse the board in Starbucks. "Caramel macchiato, please."

"I said no and discreetly nodded a yes." She grins and orders her usual.

"Damn. You know him almost as well as me."

"I'd take a chance and say I have you beat on that."

"And you can stay that way in that department," I mutter, grabbing my coffee.

"Honestly though, I thought he was gonna kill his mom the amount of times she embarrassed him." She giggles and we sink into armchairs. "I've never seen a guy before."

I smile, the caramel scent drifting up from my cup. "Braden is a serious blusher. You'd never believe it, but if you get it right you'll have him blushing like a high school freshman who just found out her skirt has been tucked into her panties all day."

Maddie snorts. "So I found out. It's cute. And, Megs . . . Did he really shave her cat?"

I choke on my mouthful of coffee and nod, hitting my chest. "I wanted a poodle, but my parents refused. Braden thought he'd be my savor and he shaved the cat. It looked nothing like a poodle, and we both ended up getting grounded for two weeks."

"His mom told me that. She also said you both spent half that time in your rooms, leaning out of your windows and yelling at passersby in the hope that she and your mom would get so annoyed they'd unground you."

The smile on my face widens as I remember. Our houses are set so they face each other, both with huge yards wrapping around. We both had the side rooms, the ones that faced the main street, and we'd lean out of them talking to each other all day until someone walked past. Then we'd shout and scream about how we'd been locked away unfairly by an evil witch.

Needless to say, I wasn't allowed to watch *Sleeping Beauty* or read *Rapunzel* for a long time. In fact, my parents confiscated all my fairy tales for about a month. That didn't go down well. At all.

"So, did anything happen here?"

"The usual. Nothing exciting." I shift in my seat.

"In other words, Kay drank too many shots and offended someone, Lila sneaked off with Ryan, and Aston took some girl back to his room and pissed her off two hours later."

"Pretty much," I agree, choosing not to correct her about Aston. It's only a half lie, anyway ...

"And you, as always, turned down advances from the numerous hot guys and disappeared back to your room. Right?" She raises a skeptical eyebrow.

"Right."

"Braden wasn't here breathing down your neck and you didn't take advantage of that?"

"Nope." Kind of no, anyway.

"Wow." She cocks her head to the side and smiles. "You really do need to get laid."

"Wow." I mirror her movement, trying not to laugh at her. "You really do spend too much time with Braden."

She opens her mouth, pauses, and closes it again, her eyes widening. "Oh my God. You're right. He's turning me into a female Frat brother!"

"Join a sorority?"

"I don't think I'm quite sorority material. Plus a good

half of them have likely slept with my boyfriend and hate me because I'm the one that got him."

"Ah, that would be awkward."

"Mhmm."

"Where is Braden anyway? Not like him to let you leave his side," I tease her.

"Ha ha." She rolls her eyes but smiles. "He's gone to sort all his crap out. In other words, interrogate Aston and make sure he didn't pull his usual tricks and get into your pants."

Wow.

"And he thinks Aston would tell him even if he did?" My eyebrows get stuck somewhere between a frown and raising in disbelief.

"Apparently," she mutters. "Just like you'd tell me if you did, right?"

"Uh, no." I laugh, biting back the uncertainty that tried to creep into my words. Dammit.

"So you might have slept together?" Maddie's green eyes sparkle over her cup.

"No."

"Right. So you might have because you're gonna tell me no anyway."

"Maddie, stop putting words in my mouth."

"It didn't work, did it?" She pouts.

"No, because nothing happened." I bang the table. "Nothing."

Nothing anyone needs to know about. And no one needs to know, so nothing happened.

That logic works a lot better in my head than I'd imagine it would outside of it.

Chapter Six - Aston

I glare at Braden. "For the tenth fucking time, I did not sleep with Megan this weekend." But not for a lack of damn well trying.

Braden folds his arms across his chest. "She seemed more pissed at you than usual in class."

I shrug a careless shoulder. "Probably because I pissed her off more than normal on Saturday night."

Ryan grins. "She did look like she wanted to wring your balls after you spoke to her at the bar."

"Yeah well, even if she did wring them, I wouldn't have been hard pressed to find someone to kiss them better afterwards, would I?"

"Shit, man." Braden shakes his head and sits down. "Was I really this much of a fucking asshole before Maddie?"

Ry throws his cell in the air and catches it. "Yep."

"Difference with me and you, dude," I say, "is that *I* can admit I'm an asshole. You thought you were fuckin' Jesus or somethin'."

"That's because I am – behind closed doors." He grins like the smug bastard he is. "At least you didn't try it with Megan."

"I don't know why you're so worried. Megan has more brains than to give the goods to this dickhead." Ry cocks his thumb in my direction, and I flip him the bird.

"You say this, but I'm the only one here with my freedom left. Your girls have your dicks in the palms of their hands," I remind them.

"And what magical damn hands they are." Ryan snickers.

"What? You never felt a magic hand before Lila?" I throw at him. "I guess I'm the blessed one."

"Blessed with the ability to snake your way into bed with anyone you want to," Braden continues.

"Because you didn't have the same ability. I must have imagined all the half-dressed girls doing the sweet walk of shame from your bedroom."

"One day, Aston, you're gonna end up just like us."

"If I ever end up as pussy-whipped as you, please, fuckin' punch me." I snort. "But that's not gonna happen, trust me."

Being pussy-whipped means feeling – and I don't do that. I don't let myself do that. Feeling means remembering, and remembering is a load of shit. Besides, the one girl that could make me is the one girl that's off-limits.

And that's a damn good thing. If I can't have her, I can't feel for her, and if I can't feel, I can't hurt her. Because I would. Eventually. Eventually the walls would build back up, push her out, and I would fall back on the only feelings that matter.

The physical ones. The ones that involve a pair of legs around my waist.

You're just like her. It'll be all you're fuckin' good

for.

"Dude?" Ryan claps his hands once. "You there?"

"Yeah." I pull myself from my head. "Thought I saw somethin'."

"You say you won't find anyone, but you will," Braden continues. "Trust me. And it'll be the girl with balls big enough to stand up to you and put your spindly little dick in its place."

"If there's a girl that can tame me I'll welcome the challenge." I lean back. "I'd like to see someone try. Gotta feel to be tamed, boys, and I don't feel a thing except for whoever it is in my bed on a weekend."

"I didn't feel anything. Then I had to play Maddie." Braden pauses, running his hand through his hair and focusing on me. "Some things are just too real to be ignored."

"See? Pussy-whipped." I snort. "Don't you two fuckers have something better to do than sit here and tell me I need love in my life?"

"Probably." Ry grins again. "But this is way more fun."

"What's fun?" Lila asks, strolling into the room and looking at Ryan.

"Annoying Aston." He reaches for her, gripping her hands and pulling her down onto his lap.

She groans. "You do realize an annoyed Aston usually equals sex, which means there'll be a pissed off girl hounding us?"

"Really?" I sit up straight. "Girls do that?" *Well damn.*

I knew I was good, but…

Lila's eyes are as flat as her voice when she turns to me. "Yes. It's like they think that because I'm Ryan's girlfriend, I have a VIP pass inside your head. I don't, thank God, but they don't get that. They all want to know why you don't call."

"Hey, I never promise to call them. I don't offer and they don't ask. Half of them don't even leave their numbers!"

Lila raises her eyebrows, and both the guys laugh.

"They don't!" I insist. "It's not my fault. How the fuck can I call if they don't leave their number?"

"Maybe they want you to ask for it."

"If I ask for it, then they'd expect me to call."

"The problem is–?"

"I won't call. If I ask for it then they have a real reason to be pissed off when I don't."

She sighs and drops her head, looking back at Ryan. He fights his smile. "Is there no way to attach a warning to him?"

"Like what, babe?" Ryan sputters.

"'Sex addict asshole who won't call, so don't even bother?'"

"That would seriously damage my reputation!" I protest.

Lila rolls her eyes and shoves herself off of Ryan's lap. She heads toward the door, stopping and looking over her shoulder at me before she passes through. "You hardly have a stellar reputation, Aston. What you need to do is have one night with a *nice* girl. You never know – you might like it. It might change your asshole perspective on things."

"Eh, she's got a point." Braden shrugs.

"Assholes." I stand and follow her through the door, taking the stairs two at a time up to my room.

I'm so fucking done with that conversation.

I nearly had one night with a nice girl. That *almost* ruined me because I can't imagine being with anyone else other than her now. I can't stop thinking about what would have – and fucking well should have – happened after that kiss. Whenever I look at her now, I picture her lying on my bed beneath me and wrapped around my body.

The guys see the Aston I want them to see. They don't see the fucked up mess inside – they don't see the real Aston. I don't intend to show the real me to anyone. Ever.

You aren't worth shit.

I let my bedroom door swing shut behind me, pushing back the echo in my mind.

I know I'm not worth shit. I don't need a ghost from my past to remind me of that.

~

I had shivered in the corner, waiting, wondering. The thin blanket I wrapped around my body did nothing to block out the chill coming from my open window – the open window my six year old body was too small to reach.

She said she'd come back. She'd promised she would, but she took too long and he went to find her. I didn't know his name, but he said she was gonna get it this time. He was angry.

I rubbed the top of my leg, flinching and trying not to cry at the stinging pain there. It was always my fault. This time it was because Mommy took too long and I cried. I don't know who he is but I don't like him. He hurt more than the last one. He had bigger arms to hit me with.

"Mommy?" I whispered into the silent darkness. I was scared. Alone and scared. Where was my mommy? Why wasn't she home yet? I rubbed at my eyes to stop myself crying.

I wanted Mommy to come home before he did. If he came home first he would hurt me again.

"Mommy?"

Chapter Seven - Megan

"He really is an asshole," Kay says, spying Aston across the yard.

He's standing in front of a girl with more highlights than my e-reader, and she's doing her best to push up her chest into his face. He smiles slowly at her, resting his arm against the tree next to him. She twirls some hair around her finger, attempting what she thinks is a demure smile, and looks into his eyes.

"I see he took the conversation we had two days ago to heart," Lila remarks.

"What conversation was that?" Maddie asks.

"I told him he needed to find a nice girl."

"You obviously have different definitions of the word 'nice'," I say, harsher than I mean to. "Because the only thing nice about her will be when she turns around and leaves."

Kay snorts. "I freaking love it when you guys get jealous."

My head snaps round. "Who said I was jealous?"

"You're so green you're practically blending in with the grass."

"Right. Because being jealous of anyone with Aston is so likely."

Yet I am jealous. I'm pissed. I'm disgusted. And I'm even more annoyed at myself for the clenching in my chest. I knew he'd be back to his usual tricks straight away, but seeing him this close to another girl when that was me just days ago pisses me the hell off.

Seeing him with another girl when he was mine, even if just for a few minutes, is like a clawed hand reaching into my chest and ripping out my heart. Even if I walked away from that kiss.

And that's all it was. A kiss. When will I get this into my thick damn head?

Aston nods to the girls, smirks, and walks across the yard. He drops onto the ground next to me and looks at me.

"What?" My eyes flick over his face.

"Nothing."

"Did Barbie have to go get her implants adjusted or something?" I snap, shifting away from him. Ugh.

Hello, irrational Megan.

It would be easier if I could get a little box to stuff this jealousy in. We'll bundle it in with the rolling stomach and clenching heart. What a tidy little package that'd be.

"She's not my type."

"Are you gonna call her?" Lila asks.

"Yep, we're going." Maddie grabs Kay's arm and pulls her up and after her.

Aston snorts and glances at me. "No."

"Does she think you are?"

He shrugs. "How am I meant to know?"

I disguise my snort by covering my mouth with my hand. My half-annoyed, half-amused snort.

"What?" he asks.

"Nothing." I shake my head. "You get with stupid girls, y'know."

"I do, huh?" He turns his face toward me slowly, his gray eyes challenging me.

"Yeah, you do." I run a thick blade of grass between my fingers, focused on him. "If I were them, I'd be shocked if you *did* call – hey, I'd be shocked if you even text. I mean, the girl who speaks to you the day after sleeping with you would have to be something, right? Hell, the girl who speaks to you after kissing you would have to be someone pretty damn special."

"Depends when I spoke to her," he replies evenly.

"The morning after?" I vocally challenge what's in his eyes and silently send him one of my own.

You told me it meant something. I call bullshit.

"If I spoke to her the next morning, then it'd mean she's more than a fuck – or a *mere kiss*. It'd mean she meant something. That she was someone pretty damn special."

Throw my words back at me, you bastard.

I guess I lose this round.

My heart pounds painfully in my chest, twisting and scrunching as what I can never have is dangled openly in front of my face. *We* are being dangled openly, for everyone to see, but they'll never know. An open secret, a complete contradiction of itself.

"Then it's a good thing no girl has ever got that morning chat, huh?" I ask quieter, forcing the hard edge into my voice.

Gray eyes flick to my lips, making me part them and draw in a breath at the intensity in his stare. Every time. Every damn time those eyes get me.

Aston rubs his chin, studying me carefully. "Yeah, it is, isn't it?" he replies just as quietly as I did.

Lila coughs and I look away from Aston. Her eyes flick between us and I grab my bag strap.

"I have to get to class. See ya later." I get up and leave without looking back.

Lila is the teenage girl version of Sherlock Holmes. If she has any suspicion someone is up to something she'll follow your ass around until she's got to the bottom of it. If we're not careful, she'll have us figured in a heartbeat.

But, as I walk back onto the main campus, I can't stop thinking about what he said.

He said I meant something. A kiss meant more than the endless stream of one night stands he's had over the last few months. How is that possible?

Huh... It doesn't matter anyway. It can't happen. That mind-blogging, knee-quaking, heart-pounding kiss shouldn't have happened, so anything else definitely shouldn't happen.

But what if "anything else" is sex? I walked away from that once. Stupid or smart, I don't know. Yet ... what if we both want that more? And what if sex turned into more? Like a relationship ... Or love. What would happen then?

Psh. Love and Aston in the same sentence? If there

was such a thing as too many books, I might agree with Lila when she says I read too many. People don't just change and neither do their actions. I don't believe for one minute he could flip a switch and go from man-whore to a one woman man.

Knowing this makes it all the easier to fight my want for him.

But in the slim chance something did change – and we're talking very freaking slim here … There just isn't a chance on this Earth I'd be able to fight anything if he wanted me the way I do him.

~

Maddie and Lila loop their arms through mine, and I'm not surprised when we begin to head in the direction of Starbucks.

"Why do I get the feeling I'm not going to like whatever conversation we're about to have?" I groan.

Maddie shrugs. "I have no idea."

"It could be, oh, I don't know … Maybe the fact you've both grabbed me and directed me toward the 'chat room' of Starbucks?" I deadpan, looking to Lila. "And the fact Lila has that grin on her face means she's up to no good."

"Okay." Lila sighs as she pushes the door open. "Go sit down. I'll get coffee."

"This is not good," I mutter to myself. "What did she do? What did she break? Oh, hell. Don't tell me she deleted my essay from my laptop again."

"Nothing." Maddie pushes me down into an armchair and sits opposite me. "She didn't *do* anything. And you know that was an accident."

"Mmph. Well she's about to do something, and if she's buying me coffee I don't think I'm gonna like it much."

"Well, it's a 'maybe baby' situation." She taps her chin. "You're either gonna love it or hate it, but I don't think it matters–"

"Because I'm gonna do it anyway," Lila sings, setting a tray on the table in front of us.

"I'm not going to lie to you, I'm starting to get a little scared." I look between the two of them, from Maddie chewing her lip to Lila's sparkling eyes.

"Just tell her, Lila!" Maddie cries. "Before she takes that coffee and throws it on you!"

I grab my coffee and point it in Lila's direction. Nothing like making a point.

"Okay! So, I've been thinking," she begins.

"Which is never a good thing," I interrupt.

"Whatever. I've noticed you're the only single one bar Kay – and I'd never dream of doing this to her."

"Damn, you noticed I'm single?"

"She's always off with some, er, someone, I'm with Ryan, and Maddie with Braden, leaving you all alone."

"Oh no." I know exactly where she's going with this.

"So I was thinking you need a guy–"

"No."

"So then you won't be all alone. Obviously Aston is out of the question …"

Obviously. "No."

"And Braden will kick your ass if you try and set her up with anyone in the frat house," Maddie points out.

"But the frat house is only a small portion of the incredibly yummy guys in this campus. I mean, come on." Lila looks around a little and leans forward, lowering her voice. "Have you seen James Lloyd lately? Holy shit! He's in my math class and he really is hot as hell."

"Boyfriend," Maddie reminds her with a sigh. "Point is, Megs, we don't want you to feel left out."

"Have I ever said I feel left out?" I look at them both again.

"Well, no …"

"But I feel like you are," Lila presses. "And I don't want you to be. Y'know, in the name of friendship and female loyalty everywhere, it really is in your best interests to let me set you up with some hot guy."

"In my best interests or in yours?" I raise an eyebrow.

"Yours, definitely yours."

"And what if I say no?"

"Oh, that doesn't matter."

Oh no. I sit upright and my hands grip the arms of the chair as I stare at her. "You haven't, Lila. You haven't."

"She has." Maddie nods her head.

Lila grins. "You have a date tomorrow night to Mark's party."

~

I can't think of anything worse than Lila setting me up with someone. Her taste in guys is questionable. Very questionable. I've been here twenty minutes and I'm starting to feel like Harriet in Jane Austen's *Emma*. God knows Lila's matchmaking skills are on par with Emma's. They're both crap. The only thing Lila has going for her is Ryan – she figured her love life out way before Emma did.

I know every single date Lila sends me on is destined to crash and burn because of the way I feel about Aston. Of course there's no way to explain that without digging myself a giant hole. There's no way to explain every guy will pale in comparison to his cocky, self-assured smirk and forceful, needing kiss. Goddamn that kiss …

Six days, and I'm still here grasping onto a memory of what could have been. Six days, and the knowledge I did the "right" thing is slowly turning into regret for not doing the wrong thing. Knowing I did the right thing is twisting my stomach.

But who is it the right thing for? Braden?

Something might be the right thing for someone else but that doesn't mean its right for you.

Right thing or not, I'd still be here having this date. I'd still be sitting mere meters from Aston sweeping into the kitchen, pretending to give a crap about something that isn't his eyes burning holes into me.

I slam the shot glass down on the bar after emptying it. Christ, I've become that girl. Alcohol to tolerate a date.

"So," the guy opposite me says. "You look a little bored."

I laugh lightly. "No, I'm sorry. I just had a rough day, y'know?"

He nods. Shit. What's his name? Ugh, stupid frat boys are rubbing off on me. I sweep my hair to one side, smoothing it away from my face, and lean in close. "Why don't you tell me more about yourself?"

And your name. Please.

"Well, I'm majoring in Biology . . ."

And I've switched off. I don't mean to, I really don't, but science is pretty much Chinese Mandarin to me. It's too realistic; I deal with fiction. I do swoon-worthy scenes, heart stopping declarations of love, and incredible guys that give girls like me unrealistic expectations.

Disney, I'm looking at you.

I pull my glass toward me and take a drink through my straw, nodding my head and pretending to be interested in Mr. Biology. Pretending because my attention is on the dark-haired girl in standing in front of Aston. Closely. Very closely.

He picks up a bottle of beer and looks up. As if he can feel me looking at him, his eyes slam into mine. They're flat, almost emotionless, almost dead, and I go cold. Nothing. That's what I get from this. Nothing.

I smile but I don't feel it. I only feel an irrational annoyance bubbling in my stomach and that coldness from his gaze spreading through my body.

"Hey." I lean forward and place a gentle hand on Mr.

Biology's arm. "I'm so sorry, but I'm not feeling great. I'm gonna head to my dorm."

"Oh. Um, sure. I can walk you back." He makes to move.

"No!" I take a deep breath. "No, I'm okay, thank you. It's not too late."

"Oh, sure."

"Thank you for a nice evening." I smile weakly and get up, spinning around.

Nice, Megan? Is that all you have? God.

My lack of convincing adjectives aside, I need to get the hell out of this frat house.

He – Aston Banks – is taking me over. He's grabbing hold of me and shaking me like a martini.

I push open the front door and step into the mild California evening air. I take a deep breath, heading back to the dorm room with a hasty step.

I need to make like Cinderella at midnight.

Chapter Eight - Aston

Time goes too fast. Too fucking fast.

Since I kissed Megan, I've slowly retreated into my own mind. Every day brings a fresh set of memories, slicing open a fresh set of scars. Every day cuts open a new wound that bleeds for hours. Every set of memories starts a fresh onslaught of cuts inside my mind that will never heal. Each one has its own shape, its own meaning, its own pain.

Each one is a reminder of why I can't give Megan what she deserves. Each one is a reminder why I should have stayed away from her in the first place and why I should now.

Broken. Shattered. Mismatched.

They're the first three words I think of when I have to describe myself. They spring to mind instantly.

Useless. Worthless. Nothing.

They're the next three. The words that were drummed into my mind so many times, by so many voices, for so long. They're the words that creep under your skin, worm their way into you and never leave.

A good word can linger with you for a few fleeting moments while a bad one will never leave.

It's too close to the words that both shattered and made my life. The words that broke and saved me.

She's gone.

I rub the heels of my hands in my eyes, bending

forwards, and take a deep breath. This … Thinking of her this weekend, the woman who was supposed to protect me no matter the cost, is inevitable, I know. That doesn't mean I want to. It doesn't mean I have any fucking intention of remembering the woman I have to call my mother.

I stand abruptly, storming across the room and yanking open my door. I leave it to slam behind me as I fly down the stairs to where music is pounding for a sophomore, Mark's, birthday party, and grab a bottle of beer from the fridge. I uncap it, raising the rim to my lips and letting the cold liquid run down my throat. I need to forget. I don't care who I forget with, I just need to forget all the shit of before.

It'd be a lot fucking easier if Megan Harper hadn't ruined me for all other girls. It would certainly be a lot fucking easier if I wasn't comparing all girls' lips to the soft, rosy pinkness of hers, or their eyes to the never-ending blue of hers.

Yeah. It'd be a lot easier if last weekend had never happened.

I catch the gaze of a girl across the kitchen. Her dark eyes give me a once over, and she flicks her black hair over her shoulder curving her lips into a smile. I lean against the end of the bar, taking in her slim figure. She saunters over to me confidently and gives me a dazzling smile.

"Can I help you?" I smirk, twirling the beer bottle between my fingers.

She steps closer, and my eyes drop to her chest. Her

boobs are almost spilling from her top, black lace creeping up above the neck of her shirt.

"I'm not sure," she says in a sultry tone. "But I'm pretty sure I can help you."

She trails a fingertip down my arm, leaning in even closer. Woah – I'm all for forward girls, but this chick has never heard of personal space.

I step back slightly. "And how can you do that?"

"Wouldn't you just like to know?" She runs her tongue across her top lip in a move I'm sure she thinks is sexy, but it just isn't doing it for me tonight.

I catch the bob of a blonde head over her shoulder and flick my eyes there. Megan downs a shot and slams the glass on the table, glancing over her shoulder and glaring at the girl in front of me. The guy next to her says something, and I hear her laugh softly, the sound riling me. She leans in closer to him, smoothing her hair round to one side. Her legs are crossed on the stool, her tight black skirt riding up the smooth skin of her thigh.

The thighs I want wrapped around my neck and my waist.

I drink a little, ignoring the girl in front of me, and watch as Megan purses her lips around a straw.

The lips I want against mine.

Her hand runs through her hair, fluffing it up and letting it fall down in a messy style.

The hand I want to thread my fingers through while I hold her under me, messing up her hair in a totally different way.

God. Fucking. Damn.

She glances back over her shoulder, her blue eyes icy as they meet mine. She smiles but there's nothing genuine about it. Her head turns, and she says something to the guy before she disappears through the crowd.

I give my attention to the girl in front of me, not really seeing her. "Look, babe, you're not really my type. Try that guy at the other end of the bar. He looks like he could use some of your help." I nod to the guy Megan was just talking to and take off, leaving the girl disgruntled behind me.

I leave the frat house, the air outside getting colder as Berkeley slowly moves into winter, and cross the street to the main campus – and the girls' dorms. Thanks to her sharing with Lila, I know her building and her room number and I know that's where she'll be.

I'm not thinking about what I'm doing. I'm not thinking about who this could hurt, what could happen after this, or even how I'm gonna feel. All I can think about is Megan and her helping me forget.

If I can't forget about her, I need to forget my past *with* her tonight.

Tomorrow, I'll deal with the shit fallout that's bound to come. I'll deal with the crap in my head from yet another bad decision.

I wink at the pair of girls that let me into her dorm block and take the stairs two at a time to her floor. I knock on her door twice and lean against the door frame.

"There's no one here," she shouts.

I bang again. "Open this fucking door, Megan, or so help me, I'll break it down."

The lock clicks and it creaks open. She pokes her face through the gap. "What the hell are you doing here?"

I nudge her into the room and shut the door, turning to twist the key in the lock. Her room is tidy, a stark contrast to the mess of mine, and it's so Megan. Books are piled high on her desk, both schoolwork and otherwise, and although she's hiding it, I can see the stuffed toys under the bed. Clothes are strung over the chair in the corner, and judging by the tidy bed next to it, I'm guessing they're Lila's.

"Hello, Aston? What the hell are you doing here?" she repeats.

I look down at her and run my hand through my hair. "Honestly? I have no fucking idea."

"Was that girl not "your type?" Her boobs too far inside her top for you?" Megan raises her eyebrows.

"Jealousy isn't a good look on you, Megs." I spin so I'm right in front of her and her back is against the door.

She tilts her head up, looking at me defiantly, and her shirt slips off her shoulder slightly. "I'm not the one who looked like they wanted to rip someone's head off at that party."

I flatten my hands on the door either side of her head, boxing her in, and move my face toward hers. My eyes search the blue in front of me. "And I'm not the one who looked like they wanted to rip out someone's extensions," I say quietly. "Who's the jealous one, Megan?"

"You," she whispers. "I have nothing to be jealous of."

"You're right." I drop one of my hands to her waist, flexing my fingers. She clenches a fist, looking at me steadily. "You don't have anything to be jealous of, because I'm here and not there."

"And why exactly are you here?"

I stare at her, barely breathing, not moving, and the words burn their way up my throat with a feral need to get out.

"Because I need you. I need to feel you again. One kiss … One poxy little kiss … It wasn't enough. It was nowhere near fucking enough, Megan. It won't ever be enough, not with you. I don't know if anything will be enough."

Her lips part slightly and her body relaxes a little. Her chest heaves as she takes a breath in. "You …" She swallows, putting a hand against my chest. "You shouldn't be here."

"I shouldn't be, but I am."

"This is wrong."

"Yep." I bend my head toward hers. "But I'm here, Megan. Think whatever the fuck you wanna think, but I'm not going anywhere until I get to kiss you senseless again."

"I'm not blind, Aston. There's more than just kissing on your mind."

"I'm not denying that."

She pauses and closes her eyes for a second. "You … Argh!" She opens her eyes. "You need to go. I can't …"

"Can't what?"

"I can't stand here with you looking at me like that and not do something I'm going to regret."

I cup the side of her head and stroke my thumb down her cheek. "You already have though, haven't you? You regret walking away last weekend. I can see it."

"No."

"If you didn't regret it you would have kicked me out by now. You wouldn't have even let me in here." I tilt her face up. "You know why I'm here and you did before you opened that door."

Her blue eyes are fixed on mine, and whatever it is she's doing to me wrecks me a little more. Whatever fucked up hold I've allowed this girl to have on my fucked up self has just strengthened a little more.

"Why are you here?" She demands.

"You know."

"Tell me. God dammit, Aston. Don't hint with me. Don't stand there, pull your usual tricks and think I'll fall into your lap with my knickers down. If you're here for a reason then you tell me now. Are we clear now?"

"Fine," I whisper, dipping my head so my face is so close to hers you couldn't get a breath between us. I can still see her eyes, though, and they're raging. "Because it obviously isn't fucking obvious enough – I'm here because I want to finish what we started last weekend. I want to push you into this wall, kiss the crap out of you, then I wanna throw you on your bed and kiss the crap out of the rest of your body. And then, Megan, then I'm gonna sink so deep inside you you'll forget where you end and I begin."

She swallows, her eyes widening. Her tongue darts out and licks a trail across her lips, sending all the blood in my body down to my cock.

I lean my body into her. "Are we fucking clear *now*?"

Megan crashes her lips into me, hot and hard. Her fingers dig into my shoulders and her body presses against me, molding to the shape of me. I kiss her harder, making her lean into the wall even more, and I'm straining through my jeans with the force of my need for her.

I move my hands across her body like I'm starved, which I am. I touch and hold, smooth and grip, probe and tickle. I sweep my tongue into her mouth, deeply, desperately, needing and wanting to taste every inch of her mouth. Her back slams into the door, and she whimpers.

Her bottom lip is soft and swollen between my teeth as I tug on it slightly, and groan breathlessly as I release it. She opens her eyes, the heaviness of her lids adding to the fire raging in them. My gaze is steady, my grip on her anything but. I hook my fingers under her shirt, shaking slightly, resisting the urge to rip it away from her beautiful skin. Her heavy breathing races between her lips, and we're so close I can almost taste it.

"Megan," I whisper, my heart pounding. I know how bad this is. I know nothing good can come from this. Three days ago she was cursing me, hating me, and now she's pinned against her door by me. I embody everything she hates.

But I don't give a shit right now. I need her. I need her so fucking badly it scares me.

Her hands slide across my shoulders and up my neck to the back of my head where she sinks her fingers into my hair, winding it round them. "Don't," she breathes out. "This is wrong. So wrong. But I can't stop myself. I can't stop this time."

Air rushes from my lungs at her words, and I take her mouth with mine harshly. Her tongue slides across my lips, wriggling slightly at the seam of them. I slide mine out, caressing hers, and I stroke my hands up her back, pulling her from the door slightly. Her kiss is demanding, asking and telling me what she wants at the same time.

I'm powerless to deny her it.

I'm powerless to deny her anything.

~

Megan picks herself up on shaky arms and legs, and I don't want to let my arms drop away from her the way they do. She grins at me, grabs her clothes, and heads for the small bathroom to the side of her room.

I push myself up onto my elbows, letting my head drop forward for a second, accepting the reality of the situation. The reality being that I am well and truly fucked – and not just in a physical sense. I'm fucked in every way possible.

I shove myself upwards, roll off the condom, and dump it in the trashcan. I wipe myself off with some tissue and get dressed. I'm just about to pull my shirt over my head when I hear the door open and Megan speak in a small voice.

"We have to go and pretend, don't we?" She looks at me, her face earnest. "We have to go pretend this never happened. Just like last time. But worse." She drops her eyes to the floor.

I pull my shirt over my head as I cross the room. I stop just in front of her, taking a deep breath.

"Yeah. That's the general idea."

She sighs heavily, dropping her hand from the doorknob. "I figured as much."

"But it doesn't mean we don't have to pretend we don't exist." I touch her waist before she can move, and she turns her face up to me, her brow furrowed.

"What?"

"I don't feel like getting my ass kicked by Braden, but for some crazy reason me walking out of here without me knowing you'll still be here drives me fucking insane," I admit, holding her gaze. "I won't leave here without you promising me you'll still be here, Megan."

"Here for what? Sex? 'Cause I can get that anywhere, Aston. It's not exclusive to you," she snaps, pushing me away. "I'm not gonna do that."

I grab her back to me, holding her against me. I lower my mouth to her ear and feel the slight tremble in the way she's holding herself.

"I said I needed you tonight. I never said it was just sex. Assuming, Megan. We all know what happens then."

"Yeah, but you're already an ass, so I didn't think it would make much of a difference."

My jaw tightens. "Face it, baby, you need me as much as I need you. Maybe I need you more. I haven't figured that out yet, but believe me, Megan Harper, if I have to walk out of this room without you promising me you're mine, I will come back and chase you down. I will chase you down and if I have to, I will pin you and your naked, trembling body to that damn bed until you say it."

She heaves in a breath and shivers. Her body relaxes against mine slightly as she wraps her arms around my waist.

"I'll be here," she says into my chest. "I don't know . . . I don't know if there was any chance I wouldn't be."

I tilt her face up and press our lips together. I could regret this. I *will* regret this. Because she makes me feel. She makes me feel human again, like a person instead of like an empty, soulless shell. She makes me feel real, even if it's only for a short time while I'm with her.

I nip her top lip. "Good," I say against her mouth. "Because I was seriously debating the bed pinning."

She smiles. "Maybe next time."

Chapter Nine - Megan

My bed smells like him, and I'm being a total teenage girl by snuggling under the covers instead of getting up. It's a spicy scent that's so out of place in California, but so right for him.

I feel a little like Juliet right now, secretly in love and holding onto it desperately. Of course that's probably much more suitable for a thirteen year old to do than me, but I'll take it because it's all I have.

The idea of telling Braden crosses my mind. Why not? That's the decent thing to do – the right thing to do. I should just tell him and get it over with. He'll probably ignore me for a few days and okay, punch Aston, but surely that would be easier than pretending?

No, it wouldn't. Telling him would mean admitting that both of us lied about last weekend – kind of. A lie of omission. Telling him would just cause unnecessary pain for all of us. It would tear Braden up and it would tear Aston and me apart before we'd even been together.

But are we even together? I have no idea. No point in telling Braden until I'm completely, absolutely sure, right? There's no point in getting him annoyed over something that might not even be.

Yes. That makes me feel better. A little.

Relationships are shit. They're so much easier to comprehend when they're not real. They make much more sense when I'm lying in bed with my covers over my head, a torch in hand and sneaking another chapter.

I snapped off the torch and lay down as Mom opened the door. "Well? Has Jo realized it yet?"

I took a few deep breaths.

"Megan Harper, you're the worst pretend sleeper this side of the Pacific, so give it up." She turned on my light, and I sat up.

"Why doesn't she get it, Mom?" I held the book up.

"Jo was a tomboy. She wanted to be fighting with her father, not sitting pretty and looking for a nice man to marry."

"I know that!" I sighed. "Laurie is so in love with her and she's blind to it. And anyway, it's not like she went looking for him. She found him by accident."

Mom laughed quietly and a smile crept onto her face. Her blue eyes regarded me with tenderness and an understanding of my frustration.

"Oh, Meg," she said softly. "The best kind of love is the kind that happens by accident."

I smile at the memory and breathe in deeply, taking one last smell of Aston, and climb out of bed with my selfish decision made. I beat back the guilt bubbling up and step into the shower. The hot water runs over my body, alleviating the tightness from my shoulders. But not the tension. That's still there – but that tension is inside, somewhere the relaxing pounding of the water can't reach.

I climb from the shower and dress quickly, shoving my wet hair up on top of my head with a few clips. The dorm is still quiet, and I expect the only person up in the Frat house will be Lila – if only because she spends more time there than in our dorm room.

My arms hug my jacket tighter around my body as I cross from the main campus to the house. The temperatures are quickly dropping and it's obvious. It's a far cry from Southern California, that's for sure.

I grasp the door handle tightly and pull open the door at the same time it's pushed from the inside. I squeak a little, jumping. Two hands land on my arms, hands I know. I look up straight into gray eyes.

"Careful," Aston mutters with a smile, rubbing his thumbs across my arms.

"What are you doing up?" I ask. I've never seen him out of bed before eleven unless he has class.

"Going for a run. I can do that, can't I?" He raises an eyebrow, still smiling, and drops his arms. His palms brush my arms and his fingers trail along in their wake. Goose pimples rise as if it was skin on skin, and my breath catches slightly. His fingertips brush mine as his hands fall away from me completely.

"Of course," I manage and decide to ask my next question silently. "Is anyone else up?" I mouth. He nods. "I'm just surprised you're up this early. I mean, aren't you usually recovering from whatever you dragged upstairs with you last night?"

A muscle under his eye twitches, and it actually hurts me to say it.

"Oh, last night was different to every other night," he says in his cocky voice. The eyes fixated on mine are softer than the edge in his tone. "In fact, I don't think I'll be forgetting it any time soon."

"I'll leave you to your remembering then." I step to the side, fighting the urge to reach for him the way I did last night.

He moves in closer, his lips brushing my ear. "Good choice."

I watch him over my shoulder as he runs off. His shirt is clinging to his body, his legs strong as they beat against the pavement.

Running - that explains that lickable washboard of abs he has going on.

"If he pulled that shit around Braden, his ass would meet the sidewalk."

I turn around abruptly, coming face to face with Maddie. She's leaning against the banister casually, her eyes on me.

"In fact," she continues. "I'm surprised you didn't put him on his ass."

"What's the point?" I shrug and enter the house. "It wouldn't bruise his overly large ego any, neither would it slice some of it off."

"Never stopped you before."

"I'm learning to pick my battles."

"And putting an egotistical, arrogant asshole on his

ass isn't one of your battles?"

"Nope. Not anymore." I slide onto a stool in the kitchen and look around. "Wow. This place was trashed last night."

"You have no idea." Maddie starts up the coffee machine. "So let me guess – Braden was the last egotistical battle you fought?"

"No. I didn't fight that – I merely passed him on to you." I grin.

"Talking about me again, girls?" The topic of our conversation strolls into the room wearing just a pair of sweatpants. He tosses his shirt at me as he passes. "I would have thought you'd be doing something productive. Isn't that usually what you two do?"

"Ew. Put that on!" I chuck his shirt back at him. "I don't want to see you half-naked this early in the morning. In fact, I'm pretty sure I don't ever want to see you half-naked."

Braden grins and pulls his shirt over his head. "You're just jealous because you don't have a kickass body like mine." He wraps his arms around Maddie and pokes his tongue out at me.

I poke back. "I don't want a body like yours. I'm happy with the girls, thanks very much. You can keep your show-off muscles. And by keep, I mean keep them under your shirt, Bray."

Maddie rolls her eyes and wriggles out of his hold. "I don't know how I cope with you two. I'd say you're like brother and sister, but that's true. You bitch like it."

"It's because despite DNA differences, we are brother and sister," Braden protests.

"And thank God for those DNA differences!" I take the cup of coffee Maddie offers.

"I agree. Fuck knows what I would have done had I ended up anything like you."

I purse my lips. "Watch it, Carter. I know all your dirty little secrets, remember?"

"And I know yours." He waggles his eyebrows.

No you don't.

"I don't *have* any dirty little secrets. You made sure of that."

"Damn right I did. But you think I don't know about Sam Carlton in senior year. I do."

I tilt my head to the side. "So that's where his black eye came from."

"Damn right."

"Are you for real?" Maddie looks at Braden. "You gave him a black eye because Megan had sex with him?"

"No. I gave him a black eye because *he* had sex with *Megan*," Braden explains. "There is a difference."

I sip my coffee, and Maddie blinks at him. "You really have been reincarnated from the Stone Age, haven't you? Did you get your big club and swing it at him? Maybe you rode up on the back of a sabre tooth tiger, growling at him?"

I snort, covering my mouth with my hand so I don't spray coffee everywhere.

"There's only one club that gets swung around

here-"

"Uh-uh." She holds her hand up. "Don't get sexual on me, Braden Carter. No wonder Megan is so uptight. She's not getting any because you're still scaring everyone away!"

"I am not uptight!" I squeak. And I am getting some. So there.

"I don't scare them off!" Braden argues. "I merely warn them that they could end up meeting my fist should they get her to scratch their itch ..." he finishes in a mumble against his cup.

"You've been saying that since the beginning of college?" I jump up and touch my forehead. "Oh my God, Bray!"

"Just a warning," he mumbles.

"Just a warning?" Maddie shrieks. "No wonder why out of the four of us girls she's the only one not in a relationship!"

"Hey! Kay isn't in a relationship," I point out.

"She's in a relationship with sex." Maddie shrugs. "Same difference."

"I haven't warned anyone since ..." Braden pauses.

"Since we went to your parent's and you told every guy in this house if they touched her, you'd personally castrate them," Maddie offers.

"Well, yeah. Then." He lowers his mug and nibbles at his thumbnail. "It's the thought that counts, right?"

I narrow my eyes at him and lower myself back to the seat. I can't believe he's actually done that. I knew he was protective of me, but holy shit! This is a whole new level.

This is cementing that what happened with Aston and I has to stay a secret for as long as possible. However uncertain "we" might be. I can feel the heaviness of the thought solidifying in my mind, getting stronger and stronger until it's a certainty.

"You do realize I can take care of myself, right?" I question him. "You do realize I'm not nine years old on the monkey bars anymore?"

"I know," he replies in a slightly softer tone, turning to look at me. "I just don't want anyone to hurt you, Meggy. You're my best friend. I want you to find the perfect person to fall in love with."

"What if I have to have a few imperfections on the way?"

He shrugs a shoulder. "That's what I'm stopping. None of the guys here are good enough for you."

"You always said you weren't good enough for me," Maddie mutters.

"I wasn't, Angel, and I'm probably still not. Difference is, I knew I was slowly falling in love with you every day. I can't guarantee that for the asshats in this place. I want someone to love Megan as much as I love you. Hell, I want someone to love Megan as much as *I* do, and if that means I have to fight off every guy that comes calling for her until he comes along, then I will. If there's two people I'll always protect, it's you two."

Yep. I hate it and it's tearing my insides apart, but

Braden can't find out.

~

"No, Mom, I'm not falling behind."

"Well, it sounds like a lot of partying goes on at that college."

"Mom. My grades are fine."

She exhales, the phone crackling. "I believe you, Megan, I just don't like the idea of my baby girl getting herself pregnant by a horny teenage boy."

"You've been watching too much TV."

"Well, that '16 and Pregnant' is on just about everywhere these days. It worries me."

My lips curve. "No getting pregnant, Mom."

"Well, at least you're using protection."

"I never said I was having sex."

"That will please your father," she says in a chirpier voice. "Talking of your father, we're off to dinner tonight so I need to go."

"Okay. Have fun, and give Dad a kiss from me."

"I will, Megs. You behave yourself."

"I always do," I reply dryly. "Bye, Mom." I hang up and drop my phone on the bed, shaking my head. Honestly. It's times like this I remember why I came to Berkeley in the first place.

Close enough to visit, far away enough for freedom. Far away enough not be the perfect little girl I was always expected to be. Granted, I failed that majorly as a kid.

I change into a tank top and bed shorts, ready to settle on my bed with some schoolwork. Mom may believe there are parties every weekend and she may be right there, but it doesn't mean I'm at every party every weekend. Just one a weekend.

I blow out a long breath, ready to tackle the English essay awaiting me, and sit Indian-style. A knock sounds at my window before I can start, and I frown. My window?

I crawl over my bed and push open my curtain and–

Stare right into Aston's face.

He grins.

"What the?" I push the window open. "Just … What?"

"Open the window before I fall out of this fucking tree!" he mutters, still grinning. I open it fully and sit back. He looks around quickly before hooking his leg over the windowsill and launching himself into my room. He falls face first onto the bed, and I lean over his legs to pull the window and curtains shut.

"Um," I say as he gets up.

"What?" He kicks his shoes off and sits in front of me.

I look at the window and back to him, pointing between them both in confusion. "Did you actually just climb up a tree and through my window?"

"Yep."

"Why?"

Aston puts his hands flat either side of me and leans forward, the tip of his nose barely touching mine. "Because I wanted to come see you."

I raise an eyebrow, not moving. "Mhmm."

"So since this whole thing is secret I thought I'd pull some ninja moves. I always wanted to be a *Teenage Mutant Ninja Turtle*, y'know." He leans forward, pressing his lips to mine, and I smile at his touch.

"Who were you?"

"Who was I?"

"Which turtle were you? Don't you know you were defined by your choice of turtle?"

He sits back a little, his head tilted to the side. "Really?"

I nod. "Oh, yeah. You had to be the right turtle, or you weren't cool at all. Who were you?"

His brows draw together slightly as he frowns. "Donnatello."

"You were cool." I press my hand to his cheek and smooth out the wrinkle in his forehead. "Why did you frown?"

"I don't remem … I was thinking." He shakes his head a little and takes my hand from his face, linking his fingers through mine. He looks at our clasped hands for a second, turning them slightly. His palm is rough and his hand is a lot bigger, almost encompassing mine completely.

Silence stretches between us for a second, and I flick my eyes up to his. He's frowning again, his light gray eyes darker. His lips are pursed and his grip on my hand tightens, making me flex my fingers.

"Aston?" I ask softly, my free hand hovering between

us, unsure of whether or not to touch him. I want to. A part of him looks vacant, so incredibly lost it's not even there, and I want to grab him and keep him in together.

He loosens his grip on my hand and focuses his eyes on mine. "Sorry … I just … Thought of something. It doesn't matter."

"Are you okay?" I shuffle a little closer to him, my hand deciding to rest against his neck.

He nods. "I'm … Fine."

I pull his face down to mine and touch my mouth to his softly. His hand snakes to my back, pulling me against him, and I find my body flush against his. He leans me back, slowly lowering my body against my bed, and lies over me. I run my foot along his leg as he runs his tongue through my mouth, kissing me the same way he did last night.

Deeply. Desperately.

And he pulls away, resting his forehead against my shoulder briefly, and he takes his hands from mine. He shoves himself up and walks across the room without a word.

What? What just happened?

I sit up, my confused eyes on him as he presses his hands against his forehead and takes a few deep breaths. "Aston?"

"I won't do it," he mutters, digging his hands into his forehead. "I won't do it."

So many things are going around my mind I don't even know if I can put them into words. I'm staring at him and his hunched shoulders, his tensed muscles, and I have no idea what he means.

"Do what?" I ask quietly.

"I won't … Use you. Not like that. Not. That. Way. Not anymore." He drops his hands and exhales raggedly. "Not you." His hands are shaking by his sides, and as if he knows I can see it he clenches his fists.

I stand and quietly move across the room, stopping just behind him. I wrap my hand around one of his clenched fists and lean my cheek against his shoulder, my other hand wrapping around his front. I splay my fingers against his stomach, feeling his whole body heave as he takes deep breaths. He drops his head back against my shoulder, turning his face into my hair, and shudders.

This is a side I've never seen. Granted, I've never seen the side of Aston that climbs through a window, either, but this … This feels like a stranger. This feels like an Aston that should only exist in a parallel universe. This feels like nothing I ever imagined he could be.

Only I don't know what he is. I thought he was a "get what you see and see what you get" kinda guy. Now I think I was wrong. Now I think – no, I know – there's a side to him he's never shown anyone, that he keeps buried deep inside. Judging by the tightness of his body, the pounding of his heart, and his slightly erratic breathing, it's a side he doesn't want shown.

But it's a side I want to see. A side I want to know. A side a part of me wants to fix, because something tells me it's a side that's a little bit broken.

Chapter Ten - Aston

You're worth nothing. You're no better than your whore of a mother.

Her body against mine. Hand on hand. Skin on skin.

You think anyone will ever want you, you brat? They won't.

The softness of her hand against mine.

You are nothing.

The gentle aroma of vanilla that's settling on her hair.

No one will want you. Megan. *You're no better than her.* I'm not there. *Little rat.* I'm here. With Megan.

Megan.

The warmth of her body against my back grounds me, holding me in the now when all my mind wants to do is give in and go back. Give in and go back to the time of my life I don't want anyone exposed to. The time I don't want Megan exposed to.

I know I need to leave. Now. I need to push her window open and climb down that fucking tree.

Instead I turn and hold her to me.

My hands splay across her back, my fingertips digging into her skin, and she wraps her arms around my waist. Her face presses into my neck and she brushes her lips across my collarbone, a feather light touch. My grip tightens on her and I push my face into her hair again, the ends tickling my nose. I shake my head slightly, holding her ever tighter.

Sex. Sex doesn't hurt – it can't hurt anyone. *It's all you'll be good for.* My fall back and way of coping. *Just like her.* The thing that keeps the demons at bay and stops them clawing at the corners of my mind.

This weekend, thirteen years since Mom died, the demons are stronger than ever. The memories of that weekend flood my mind and there isn't anything I can do to stop them.

Except hold Megan.

I have no idea what it is about her, but I know that I need her. And I know that for all my forgetting over the years, she makes me remember. For that, I should push her away. I should run away screaming.

But the pain from remembering is nothing compared to the softness of her touch when she takes that pain away.

And that's why I won't use her, not in the way I've become so accustomed to.

I breathe in deeply and turn my face toward Megan's, nuzzling the side of her head with my nose. "Lila will be at the house tonight?"

She nods against me. "Always on a weekend." Her hands rub along my back in a soothing motion, slipping under my shirt, her hands like silk against my skin. Her fingers probe gently, coaxing my clenched muscles into relaxation.

"I want to stay," I whisper. "Let me stay."

She pulls back, taking one hand from my back and

running it around my body. It climbs up my stomach and chest, finally resting against the side of my face. I open my eyes to meet her wide blue ones, the soft safety of them drawing me in.

"Of course," she replies quietly. "Whatever you need."

I let out a shaky breath. "I just need to be with you."

Megan reaches up on tiptoes and kisses me softly. "All night?"

I can't miss the wariness of her tone, two simple words riddled with uncertainty. My hands frame her face and I rest my forehead against hers.

"All night."

Just Megan.

We move back to her bed and climb under the covers. Her body tucks into mine perfectly, my arms circle her like they were made to, and my heart pounds to a beat only she can hear.

My fucked up coping mechanisms are trying to take over and it's hard not to give in. Hell, I want to watch her give herself over to me. I want to watch her body arch and feel her muscles tighten as she lets go. I want to see the sparkle in her eye, hear the cry leave her body, feel her nails in my back.

But I have to remember it's Megan. She's more than any other girl. She's something I don't deserve yet, something I can't give up.

I pull her tighter to me and bury my face in her hair. The soft strands tickle my face and I breathe in deeply. She stretches an arm over my stomach and threads her legs through mine, tangling us together, and leans her head back to kiss my neck softly.

In this moment she is mine. She might not be tomorrow, next week, next month, but right now … She's fucking mine.

So I let myself hold her, wondering if there's a chance she'll ever know the peace she brings me.

~

Megan eyes me speculatively. "I have a question."

"It's never good when you have a question." I grin.

"It's not that bad!"

"Oh, yeah? Like that time in English when you promised it wasn't a big question and kept the prof talking for half the class?"

She shrugs a shoulder, smiling a little. "Hey, it made for an easy class!"

I lean forward, putting my face to hers. "And a fuck off essay after."

"Um, yeah." She smiles cutely, wrinkling her nose. "Anyway …"

"Go on, then." I hope to shit she doesn't ask–

"Yesterday, when I asked which turtle you were." Shit. "You … You seemed to go somewhere else. Like … You had no idea what I was talking about."

I sit back, words and excuses swirling in my mind. "I was home-schooled," I answer tentatively. "So I never really knew all that stuff. My Gramps taught me."

"Your Gramps? Why not your mom? Or dad?"

Of all the days she asks me today. She asks me on the one day I can't talk about it.

"I can't . . ." I get up. "I can't have this conversation today, Megs. Any day but today."

"He's in here somewhere."

I had moved further into the corner of my bedroom, hugging my blanket tighter. Mommy still wasn't home. I was still waiting, and now some funny lady was in my house talking about "he". Was she here for me?

No. I didn't want to leave Mommy. They always said it would happen, the big men. They always said that one day they would take me from my mommy.

I covered my face with my hands so they couldn't hear me breathing and slipped under my bed. I moved back to the darkest corner, shaking and trying not to cry.

I don't want to leave my mommy. I don't want them to take me away.

My bedroom door opened, and I shook harder. No. Don't let them find me. Please. The light flicked on, and I could hear their footsteps across my bare wooden floor. I could see the shadows as they walked further.

"Have you checked under the bed?" one woman asked.

"No. I'll do that."

Nononononono. Don't find me. Please don't find me.

A kind face appeared and morphed into a gentle, coaxing smile. The woman held out her hand. "Come on now, honey. Let's get you out of here."

I shook my head, shrinking back further. "I want Mommy," I whispered.

"I don't have her, sweetheart, but I can help you. You're shaking, are you cold?"

I nodded.

"I have a nice thick blanket here for you. And some cookies – you like cookies?"

"Cookies?" I frowned.

"Yes. They're really yummy and these ones have chocolate chips. Would you like to try one?"

I had no idea what she was talking about, but I was hungry. I scooted forwards a little bit. "A cookie?"

"Yes. Come out from under your bed, we'll get you warm and you can have a cookie. Okay, Aston?"

"You know my name?" I bit my lip, my eyes wide, and moved back a little.

"Yes, I'm here to help you. I won't hurt you, I promise. We can be friends, yeah, buddy?" she asked softly.

She wasn't a man. She didn't look horrible. I couldn't see any pictures on her skin and she didn't smell like the men.

I shuffled across the floor and out from under the bed. Another woman was standing there and I flinched away as she moved closer.

"It's okay, sweetheart. I'm giving you this blanket to

keep you warm." She smiled encouragingly, and I took the blanket, not wanting her to touch me.

The other woman bent down and looked me in the eye. I clutched Bunny tighter to me.

"How about that cookie?"

I nodded, climbing onto my bed. She reached into her purse and pulled out a red shiny packet. She opened it and pulled out a round, light brown circle with dark spots on. I took it from her tentatively, still scared of her. My eyes were flicking between the two women in front of me, being nicer to me than anyone ever had before.

"Try it," the first woman coaxed. "Just a little bite?"

I brought it to my mouth and nibbled at a dark spot. The sweet flavor exploded in my mouth and I gasped, biting into the cookie. My stomach rumbled as the crumbs flooded my mouth. I'd never tasted anything like it. It was the best thing ever.

"My God," the second woman breathed. "The neighbors were right. The system has failed this kid. He's never even eaten a cookie at six years old."

The first woman looked at me. "Is this the first time you've had a cookie, Aston?"

"Yes," I whispered. "I like it. It's yummy."

"How about another one?"

I nodded, staring into the face of the woman who was my childhood savior.

"Just, not today." I repeat, breathing deeply as I let

the memory go. Thirteen years, and the main marker I have of this day is the first cookie I ever ate. "I need to go. I have to go see my Gramps."

Megan looks at me worriedly, sadness in her eyes, and I cross the room to her. I cup her face in my hands, rest my forehead against hers, and exhale.

"It's not you, Megs. There's a lot about me you don't know – a lot I don't want you to know. It's not nice stuff, it's not good, okay? Today isn't a day to talk about it. Maybe there won't ever be a day. I don't know."

"I want to know," she whispers, resting her hands on my arms.

"I don't want you to know." I kiss her and quickly move away. I push open her window, make sure it's clear, and jump out onto the tree branch.

"Then whenever you're ready," she whispers. "I'll be here. Waiting."

I glance over my shoulder, and she's watching me go. I make eye contact with her for a second. Set on seeing Gramps, I jump down the tree.

~

"Didn't think I'd see you today." Gramps' voice grumbles through the house.

"It's Sunday," I reply simply, crossing the front room and sinking into my usual seat opposite him.

"Ain't just any Sunday." He twists his lit cigar between his weathered fingers, staring at the smoke rising from it.

"Doesn't mean I'm not gonna see you." I watch the twirling smoke.

"Thought you didn't wanna know today."

"I don't, but I'm still gonna come see you. You need me."

"I need to look at your face and know you look exactly like her?" He puffs on his cigar, the end of it glowing bright orange. "You do, you know. You look exactly like her."

"I . . ." I drag my eyes to his and see the pain there. "I know."

"You're smart, too. Just like she was. I could tell that when I started teachin' ya. Picked up your numbers like Einstein. Of course, she was good with numbers in a different way."

The numbers of the street.

"I hate that so much of me reminds you of her."

"Why? 'Cause you hate the memories? Your memories and mine, they're different, boy. If you'd let me share mine you'd see a different side to your mom than the one you know. You'd see that she ain't all bad. She just jumped on the wrong train and couldn't get back off."

"And that's what she turned our life into. A damn train wreck. Everything . . ."

"And today is a day to remember it, however you want to."

"You think I don't, Gramps? You think I'm not haunted by the memories of the past every day? You think I don't remember? I don't want to remember it. Not at all. But I do."

"It's good to remember," he pushes on, twisting his cigar in the ashtray. "You gotta remember where you've been to see how far you've come."

Chapter Eleven - Megan

"Come on!" Kay begs. "It's Sunday. Who the fuck does school work on a Sunday?"

"I do," I tell her. "It has to be in tomorrow, so I have to do it."

"Didn't you stay in last night to do this?" She raises her eyebrow.

"Yes."

"So why didn't you do it?"

Because I was busy with my sort-of-almost-boyfriend. "Because I fell asleep early."

"You never go to sleep early."

"Oh my God! What is this? Interrogate Megan time?" I slam my pen down and look up at her. "Do you want me to tell you my turn-on spot while you're here? Shit, Kay!"

She snorts. "No offense, babe, but I'm not really into you like that, so we'll pass on the turn-on spot. But why were you asleep early?"

"Gee, I don't know, Kay. Why do people usually go to sleep? Could it be because they're tired?" I sigh.

"Shit the bed, someone is expecting Mother Nature!"

"Not for two to three weeks."

"Then you must be pregnant … Oh wait–"

"Kay? Go fuck yourself."

"I'm going," she mutters, pulling the door open. "Try not to get your panties too twisted, my little hormonal bag of joy!"

I throw my pen across the room, hitting the shut door. I stare at it blankly for a second, then shake my head. I'm actually trying to write the essay – trying being the main word in that sentence.

I'm trying and failing because my mind is stuck on Aston and the way he acted last night. And this morning.

The Aston I've always known – and the one I fell for – is cocky. Egotistical. Pig-headed. He's devil-may-care, flighty, and doesn't think about anyone else. But that wasn't the Aston I saw this morning. I could see it in his eyes – a deeper, darker part of him that makes me think his act is just that. An act. A charade put on to fool people.

A game he's playing with himself, constantly fighting for the winning spot. A game he's unwilling to lose, whatever the rules may be.

I get up to retrieve my pen and settle back on the bed, twisting it between my fingers. I have no idea why he said he needed me or why he said he wouldn't use me. I have no idea why he's acting the way he is.

Hello, he climbed through my freaking window.

Is it too much to think that – maybe – I could make him better? Whatever it might be that haunts him, whatever it is that makes his eyes darken the way they do ... Maybe I make it bearable.

But what is it about today that's haunting him so much? I wish he could have said. I wish he would have just told me.

I wish I knew if he was okay. And I wish I had the

balls to pick up my phone and find out.

But I don't.

~

"So you ran out on Charlie on Friday night, went to bed early on Saturday, kicked Kay out of the room last night, and still didn't finish the essay?" Lila raises her eyebrows.

"Yup," I sigh. "That pretty much sums it up."

She frowns, chewing on a Twizzler. "Why?"

"Because I just didn't." I shrug. "I don't have a reason. I guess I wasn't in an English essay mood this weekend."

"What kind of mood were you in?"

"Apparently, a sleeping one."

"And your excuse for running out on your date?"

"He's not my type."

"He's hot, muscular, *and* his dad is kinda rich. How can he not be your type?"

We get up from the lawn and make our way to the main building. Lila throws her empty packet in the trashcan before we pass through the double doors and hoists her bag onto her shoulder.

"That stuff doesn't mean anything to me, Li, you know that. Money is money. It talks but it lies, too. And looks are crap – the hottest guy could be the biggest asshole in the world. It just … It doesn't matter."

"Let me guess – there was no magical spark and

unrelenting passion as for Mr. Darcy and Elizabeth?"

"Absolutely," I agree, my lips twitching into a smile. "He pales in comparison to the wonderful Darcy."

"You and your books." She shakes her head.

"There's nothing wrong with my books. They give me what I don't have in real life."

"Like the perfect guy?"

"Exactly! And until I have my Mr. Darcy, I won't stop reading. Charlie was definitely not Mr. Darcy."

"You know something? You're a really bad liar," she says out of the blue.

"Hang on – what? How did you come to that conclusion when I'm not lying?"

"And again." Lila laughs. "I don't know what you're lying about, but you're not telling me the complete truth. At least not about this weekend." She stops outside her class and tilts her head, studying me. "Got anything you want to share?"

I look at her, taking in her upturned lips and curious eyes. "Nope." I hug my books to my chest. "Nothing I want to share."

I'm not lying. I don't want to share what happened in the slightest.

"I guess I'll just have to find out by myself." She grins and disappears into her class.

I take a deep breath in. See? If Sherlock Holmes and Cupid could have babies, the baby would be Lila.

An arm rests on my shoulders. "Smile, Meggy," Braden chimes, steering me toward our class.

"Where's Maddie?"

"She's in bed. She's sick."

"She better just be sick." I look at him pointedly.

"Fuckin' hell, you sound like Mom."

"It's because I learned it from her." I smile sweetly at him and push my way up the staircase, shrugging his arm off.

"You seem different."

What is it with people today? "Do I?"

"Yep."

"How?" I look at him like he's crazy and enter the room.

"You seem … Distracted? Yeah, distracted." Braden chews his thumbnail.

"I'm always a little scattered, Bray, you know this. Maybe it's just pronounced today." I shrug and slide into my seat next to Aston. Braden perches on the edge of my desk.

"Why are you still sitting next to this ass?" Braden looks at me, grinning.

I roll my eyes. "Because even sitting next to this ass is preferable to you telling me how "different" I seem today. I've had it from Lila all morning."

"Different?" Aston questions. "Different how? Hey, Megan, did you finally get some?"

Smart boy.

"Hey, Aston, I see you finally managed to get your dick back in your pants long enough to make it to class." I smile at him, exaggerating it for Braden's benefit.

"Well, you know . . ." He leans back in his seat, linking his fingers behind his head. "Sometimes it's a fucking hard call, but I thought I should probably make an appearance. Wouldn't want you missing me now, would I?"

"I'd miss you like I would a lego under my foot. Oh, wait, I wouldn't miss that!"

"Do you two even know what you sound like?" Bray looks between us.

"I have ears, Braden," I retort. "I can hear, funnily enough."

"You sound like an old married couple."

"I said I can hear."

"I know. I chose to ignore you."

"Well isn't that a surprise?"

"You two sound like a couple of kindergarten kids," Aston offers.

"You two sound like you want my knee in your balls," I say, following suit. "This is why I sometimes wonder if Kay is the smartest person I know. Guys are annoying."

Braden snorts, jumping up. "Of course we're fuckin' annoying. We have to be to put up with *your* annoying whiny asses."

I scrunch up a ball of paper and launch it at his head as he walks to his desk. It bounces off the back of his head and he bends down, scoops it up, and throws it back at me. I catch it and grin.

"He's got a point," Aston mutters.

I turn, looking at him blankly. "I meant what I said about a knee in the balls."

"You're really fucking hot when you're mad."

I swallow the bubble of laughter inside my chest and fight the smile my lips are twitching into. "I'm not mad. I can always get mad though, and when I do I'll be so hot I'll burn your damn ass."

He grins slowly – that sexy grin he does – and lowers his eyelids slightly. My heart pounds a little harder when I recognize that look as his bed look.

"Is that an offer?" he says in a low voice.

I can feel Braden's eyes on us. "Even if it was, it wouldn't be much of an offer because you wouldn't be able to pay the price."

"Try me," he offers, his smile turning cocky as we both put on the charade. As we both play for the silence of the secret we have. As we play for keeps.

For keeps of each other. For keeps of the secret that binds us together. For keeps of the lie we're now committed to telling.

The lie that breaks my heart a little every time I play this game.

I flick my blonde hair over my shoulder and smile, resting my chin on my hand, and cross my legs. "How about the price would be so high that you'd be ruined for all other girls – and you'd never have an opportunity to put it back in your pants?" My stomach twists with my own words.

He runs his teeth across his bottom lip, his gray eyes

darkening a shade as they flick down my body and back up. When he looks at me the way he is right now, I feel naked. Like he can strip away the layers of clothing I'm wearing to my body beneath with a mere glance.

"I don't think that would be such a bad price," he mutters, stretching his arms out in front of him and tapping his fingers against the edge of the table. "In fact," he says even quieter as the class finally starts. "I think I've paid that damn price."

I almost choke as I breathe in sharply. *Only I could choke on air.* Aston raises an eyebrow, and I do the only thing I can do. I spin abruptly in my seat, focusing on the front of the room. It's not what I want to do … but that's an "if only". If only. If only.

I keep getting caught up in games. First, Maddie and Braden's – and now my own, however voluntarily. Both a game for love, but each with their own set of complex yet easily broken rules. Both with the ability to make or break the players. And both with the same prize.

The one thing coveted above all else, for however long it lasts. The one thing we all want regardless of who gets broken along the way. The one thing that no matter the cost, no amount of money could ever buy it.

The grand prize we play for.

Love.

~

"I went to the supermarket and I bought an apple."

My lips curl to one side and I look behind me at Braden. "What?"

"I went to the supermarket and I bought an apple," he repeats, sitting opposite me on the picnic bench.

I know this. We used to play it all the time when we were kids – usually when we were hiding from our parents because we'd done something wrong. By the time we'd finished it, they'd forgotten we were in trouble because they were so worried.

We were the biggest little shits ever.

I close my book and resign myself to the fact he won't let it go until I play. "Okay. I went to the supermarket and I bought an apple and a beer."

He raises an eyebrow. "I went to the supermarket and bought an apple, a beer, and a crotchless thong."

"What?" I cover my face with my hands and shake my head. "I cannot believe you just said that."

I guess this game has evolved a little over the last ten years.

"You know the rules." He kicks me under the table.

"Fine. I went to the supermarket and I bought an apple, a beer, a crotchless thong, and a dildo."

He pauses before bursting into laughter. I grin at him, propping my head on my hands.

"I really wasn't expecting that," he admits.

I shrug. "Bit of a change from bananas, carrots and donuts, right?"

"Just a fucking bit." He laughs again. "For once I'm going to quit. I'm a little worried about what we could come up with."

"You and I both, Carter."

"So, Harper." He leans forward, studying me. "What's up?"

You're kidding me. I appreciate the concern, but sheesh.

"Mom set you on my case, didn't she?" I raise my eyebrows again. "She was going on about me getting pregnant this weekend."

"What the fuck?"

If the twitching of my lips didn't give me away, I so would have followed through with that.

"I'm not pregnant. She's worried about me getting pregnant."

"No. Well, yes. She did call me." He rubs his hand down his face. "For what it's worth, I reminded her you have to have sex to get pregnant, so you're definitely safe there."

This is becoming a common theme for my conversations.

"Gee, thanks," I reply sarcastically. "Was that all?"

"No. Y'know, sometimes I think about when we were kids and think we were right little fuckers."

"We were. It's a wonder our parents hadn't killed us by age ten."

"Shaving the cat ... Climbing trees ... Flushing your cousin's diaper down the toilet ..."

"That was you!" I poke his arm across the table. "I had nothing to do with that."

"It absolutely fucking stunk, Meggy!"

I'll give him that. Ever smelt a diaper done by a ten month old? They're not pretty.

"Thinking back I don't think Mom was as bothered about the toilet being blocked as she was about the mess on the sofa." I look at him pointedly.

"Damn," he mutters. "I was eight. How was I supposed to know the kid would pee everywhere? I could control that shit. I thought I always could – I didn't realize it was like a specialized skill."

The worst thing here is he's telling the truth. He genuinely didn't know my cousin would pee everywhere without a diaper on.

"I'm surprised she let you in the house again after."

"I didn't pee on the sofa." He grins. "I'm house trained."

"Oh, gee, I'll be sure to let Maddie know."

"You're cocky, Meggy."

"I learnt from the best." I smile sweetly at him as we get up.

Braden laughs, wrapping an arm around my shoulders again and squeezing me. "I miss being kids. It was so damn easy."

Me too. No work, no future to worry about, no feelings to hurt.

No lies to tell.

Chapter Twelve - Aston

"Remember where you've been to see how far you've come," I mumble to myself, pushing the psych paper aside. "Yeah alright, Gramps. Fuckin' helps if you've actually got somewhere, though, doesn't it?"

I push the heels of my hands into my eyes, rubbing harshly. Hear something enough and it'll be burned into your body, scarring your skin and tattooing itself in your mind. It doesn't matter how long ago the words were said. It just matters that they were.

Thirteen years and I don't feel like I've got anywhere. So what if I'm not the scared little boy in the corner anymore? He's still inside. He's still afraid, still shivering. He's still bruised, he's still broken, and he's still beaten.

Just because I appear not to give a fuck doesn't mean I actually don't. Not everyone is what they seem, and I'm one of those people. I don't even know who I am, because I spend so much time fighting against who I don't want to be. I have no time to be who I want to be. I have no time to be who I could be.

I spend too much time fighting against the memories that are buried deep down. But it doesn't always work – occasionally they creep up on me faster than I realize and consume me, taking me back to the place I hate more than anything. It's always voices – always whispers lingering on the edge of my consciousness. Sometimes a whisper is worse than a scream.

Just like her … No good for anything … Worthless …

I shove away from the desk, my chair getting caught on the carpet. It tips backwards as I stand. I ignore it, slip my feet into my sneakers and grab my wallet.

I need to prove them wrong. I need to prove myself wrong.

I ignore everyone on my way out of the house. If I speak to anyone, if I stop, if I think for even a second, I'll be back in my room still swirling in the same pool of fucking self-doubt.

My engine whirs to life, and I pull away from the frat house. There's a bar just outside the city, set away from the roads leading to the interstate, and it only takes one glance at the bar to know it's a run down, no ID, shabby place.

The kind of place my mom would have worked at. The kind of place she would have been picked up at. The kind of place her dead body was found at.

I push on through the city traffic full of perfect people driving back to their perfect families in their perfect little goddamn houses.

You're not worth anything.

I flick the radio to "on" and *Trapt* blares out, the beat of *Headstrong* fueling the feelings running rife through my body. A mixture of anger, determination, frustration, and a sliver of helplessness.

Because they still control my life. No matter what I do or where I go, the bastards that controlled my early childhood control me even now.

I take the turn off to the small road that will lead me to the bar. The road is deserted, no cars, nothing, until the bar comes into view. The parking lot outside is half full with rusted, run down cars that need more than a fresh coat of paint. My car looks out of place here.

I look out of place here.

I *am* out of place here. Mom wouldn't have been; this would have been her idea of heaven. Here is where she could have arranged a meeting with a rich guy – the guy that would probably pay over the odds and then some, all because of the privacy.

I pull a cap onto my head and get out of the car, staring at the exterior of the bar. The sign is slightly broken, one of the lights flickering pathetically against the darkening of the sky behind it. Eighties music hums from inside, and a woman's voice screeches. A scratchily written sign proclaims a karaoke night.

I push open the door and get hit by the smell of stale smoke and beer. A woman in a barely there outfit passes in front of me, a tray raised above her head as she weaves her way through the patrons gathered about the bar. It's far from busy, but everyone is focused on the thirty-something woman trying to sing in the corner of the bar.

I adjust my cap and order a beer. I was right. This place doesn't care about ID. A beer is put in front of me and I hand over the cash. No-one gives me a second look apart from the waitress cleaning glasses at the opposite end of the bar.

Her eyes flick up and down me and she runs her tongue across her lips. Her clothes barely cover any skin, leaving her body on show.

It's all you'll be good for.

Her bleach blonde hair is flicked over her shoulder as she bends over to put glasses away, causing every man at the bar to look at her ass.

You're just like she is.

She straightens, sending me a suggestive smile. She's not much older than me, maybe one or two years. I drink some of the flat beer as she meanders across to me.

"What's a guy like you doing in this bar?" She leans forward, resting her elbows against the sticky wood. Her tits squeeze together, almost popping from her top.

You're nothing, just like her. It's all you're good for. You're worthless. Useless. A pile of shit. You're just the son of a whore, born to be a whore.

There's no stirring in my dick, no attraction toward this waitress flaunting herself right in front me. There's no desire at all, except the one to get the hell out of here.

"You know what?" I push the glass toward her and stand. "I have no fuckin' idea."

I don't wait for her reaction, instead I turn and leave the bar within minutes of my arrival. No-one notices me getting out except her. I was invisible.

My car is comforting. I rest my head against the steering wheel, fighting against the constant voices swirling in my head.

"I'm not," I say quietly. "I'm not like her. I'm *not* like

her!"

And I'm not.

If I was, I'd be waiting for that girl to finish her shift so I could fuck the shit out of her. That's what my mom would have done, except she would have sold her body for money or drugs. She wouldn't have thought about what she was doing or how it was affecting those around her.

But I am thinking. And I'm not waiting for the waitress.

I'm driving away from the seedy, run-down bar full of everything that's bad.

I'm heading back to Megan. To something good.

~

Seeing her face, even if it is across a crowded hallway, makes the day brighter. Seeing the guy next to her, making her laugh, makes the day turn darker than the dead of night.

It drives me fucking crazy. I should be the one walking beside her, making her laugh and wrapping my arm around her shoulders. Not that fucking asshole.

I lean against the wall, waiting and watching as they come closer. She shrugs his arm off, adjusts her books and rests them against her hip. The hip that's between them. She tucks some hair behind her ear, making her face more visible to me.

Her blue eyes collide with mine for a second, but her facial expression doesn't change, and neither does mine.

Any twitch of lip, any blink of an eye, any movement of our bodies is all it would take to out us. We both know that.

The stakes of this game are high.

They're too high, and it makes me wonder if it's worth it. If it's worth the lying and sneaking around. Then I look at her. I get a glimpse into her eyes and a twitch of a smile from her, and I know there's no chance I can stop playing this fucked up game.

She drops her gaze as she walks past, and I drop mine to her ass. Her jeans hug it tightly, and I remember what it's like to hold it as she moves against me.

The more time I spend around her or thinking of her, the more I need her – the more I need the peace she can bring me. The more I need the complete and utter silence she brings me when she's tucked tight in my arms. The more I need to prove that I'm not my mom, that I'm more than a whore's son, born to be a whore myself. The more I need to prove to myself that I'm more than that – just like I did last night.

I'm not good enough for Megan. I know that. I'll never be enough for her, and it's best for her if she packs her bags and runs in the opposite direction screaming for her life. I don't know if I'll ever be able to let her in the way she wants. I don't know if I'll ever be able to tell her all of me, let her know all of my past. I don't know if the shaking little boy inside, stuck in a hall of horrifying memories will ever be able to break free from that and let me be with her completely.

But I still won't use her the way I've used girls for so

long.

I would rather lose her entirely than use her for my own selfish needs.

The halls are almost empty when the dick walking with her disappears into his class and leaves her standing alone. I grab my cell from my pocket.

You have class?

I watch her as she takes her own from her bag. *No,* she sends back instantly, leaning against the wall. I shove the phone back into my jeans and walk in her direction.

"Football field," I mutter. "Five minutes."

I can't look back to see if she responds no matter how much I want to. I just have to hope she'll get that pretty little ass down there.

I push open the double doors and almost walk into Ryan.

"Took your fuckin' time," he mutters.

"Don't start your girly shit with me today, man," I warn him. "I never said what time I'd be done."

"What? Didn't bag a girl in class to scratch your itch?"

"Why would I? You know I only pull that shit at weekends. You aren't the only one with grades to keep."

"You mean you actually have grades?"

"You're a dick, Ryan." I shake my head. "And yeah, if you must know, I graduated high school with a GPA of 3.8, so fuck you."

"Shit! That's higher than mine!" he exclaims. "I barely scraped a 3.4 to get in here from out of state! How the hell did you manage that?"

"My gramps was probably a better teacher than the poor shits that got stuck with your ass," I reply. "That's how I managed it."

"Did you not go to school at all?"

"I went the last two years, and that's it. It was easy as hell. I'd already learned most of it, so I spent it fucking about and surprising the hell out of my teachers with near perfect scores on most tests."

"I never knew that." He pushes the door open and we step into the house.

"Why would you? You all assume my brain is in my dick. Hey," I pause and shove my book in his direction. "Take these."

"The fuck?"

"I left something in class rushing to meet you. I'll be back in a minute." I spin and leave the house. All I can focus on is getting to the football field – and if I'd stayed two seconds longer Ryan would have kept me there.

When I'm out the view of the house I break into a jog, detouring around the campus buildings instead of going through them. Fucking hell, why does the damn field have to be on the other side of this place?

There's some guys running around on the field, but I can't see Megan anywhere until I scan the bleachers. She's standing under them, looking between the seats on to the field.

I smirk and silently jog to her, placing my hands on her sides. I touch my lips to the side of her neck, and she turns her face into me.

"You know," she whispers, "I feel like I'm back in high school." She spins in my hold and looks up at me.

"Who were you meeting under the bleachers in high school?" I raise my eyebrows.

"Only every guy I've ever dated. And apparently you're no exception."

"So we're dating?"

She slips her hands up my chest and clasps them around my neck, her face coming close to mine. "Unless you're in the habit of creeping through girl's windows, I'd say so."

My lips twitch on both sides. "No habit here."

Apart from her. Megan Harper is my habit and she's one I stand no chance of breaking. I have yet to decide if it's good or bad.

"Why are we here?" she asks and pauses. She smiles. "Oh. I get it. You've got a case of the caveman."

"Bullshit," I fire back, pulling her body closer to mine and kissing her. "I wanted to see you without us bitching at each other. You complaining?"

"No." She kisses me again. "But admit it, Aston. You saw Tom with his arm over my shoulders and got pissed off. That's why you text me."

Her eyebrows are arched over her amused blue eyes, her lips half-pursed and half-smiling. I stare at her for a moment and give in.

"A little," I admit. "I fucking hated seeing that prick with his hands on you."

Megan brings her hand to my head and touches my

cheek. "A lot," she corrects me. "You looked like you were ready to drag me out of there by my ear just to get me away from him. I hate to say it but you'll have to get used to it."

"Fuck that," I mutter. "If that happens much more I'm gonna stand in front of Braden and gladly take his shit for being with you. I can't fucking deal with seeing that all the time."

"You have two choices. You can see me with them and know I'm with you, or you can see me with them and wonder which one I want."

Fuck that for a laugh. I take a deep breath and lean my forehead against hers. "Fine. I'll deal with it. But I don't damn well like it, Megs."

"I know." She smiles. "I don't like it much either, but if it makes you feel better, Tom's a jackass."

"So am I," I mumble.

Her hand snakes into my hair and she holds me tightly. "Yep. But you're a special kind of jackass."

"Yeah?" I dip my head and brush my lips across her. "What kind is that?"

"My kind of jackass."

~

"It just occurred to me I don't know your major," Ryan throws at me as I walk into the frat house.

I grin, still buzzing from being around Megan, and sit down. "Psychology."

"Are you for fucking real?" He sits up.

Braden walks in, eating an apple. "Is who for real?"

"This dick is majoring in psych. Did you know that?" Ryan cocks a thumb toward me and looks at Braden.

"He can't be." Braden looks at me and I smirk. "Are you really?"

"Pretty damn sure that's why I do the classes the course requires."

"Well, fuck me." He leans against the door frame. "What you studying that for? To understand why you need so much sex?" Him and Ryan chuckle.

So I can understand why my mom was the way she was and stop other people going that route. So I can help stop other kids dealing with the shit I had to.

"I know why I need sex, asshole," I retort. "I'm doing it to work out why people like me hang around with fucktards like you two."

"Oh, that's easy," Ryan shrugs. "We make clever dicks like you look good."

"True that," Braden agrees.

Ryan looks at him. "You know something? I don't even know what your major is."

Braden shrugs a shoulder carelessly, chewing. "You know something?" He grins. "I don't fucking know either."

I laugh at the smile on his face. "Ryan, man, you might just have a point about you two making me look good."

"I'm majoring in engineering, if either of you dicks care." He shrugs.

"Hey, that's supposed to be pretty tough. All that math and stuff," Braden says vaguely.

"Math was all I could do well in school. It made sense."

"Yeah, well." Braden straightens, dropping the apple core in the trashcan. "The only math I know is that me plus Maddie, minus clothes, equals a product not even algebra can create. Shame we can't major in sex. I'd walk away top of the class."

I smirk as he leaves with a satisfied smile on his face, and Ryan snorts.

"That's some pretty sweet math … One I think this whole house can appreciate." He grins.

I nod in agreement, thinking of Megan.

Fucking right I can appreciate that.

Chapter Thirteen - Megan

I must be the only person in my class that will read a classic novel for anything other than requirement. I can't think of anyone I know that would pick up *Jane Eyre*, *Little Women*, or *Tess of the D'Urbervilles* for pleasure.

In fact, they're not even my first choice. *Little Women* comes in a close second, but *Pride and Prejudice* will always win out. There's something beautiful about a couple from two different backgrounds traveling along the bumpy road of love until it's undeniable, and there's something even more beautiful about watching that journey happen. Flicking through the pages anxiously waiting for that sweet first kiss, the passion filled argument, the final declaration. There's something that pulls me in and takes me away from the real world.

There really is no place like the one you find between the pages of a book.

The only place that comes close is in the arms of the person you love.

Perhaps that's why with Braden in class all day, I'm sitting on the corner of Aston's bed reading – and swooning over – the beauty that is Mr. Darcy. I'm pages away from one of the best scenes in the book – the rain scene where everything is so passionate and wet and *oh my God, get together already!* And I'm not ashamed to admit it, but I'll happily yell at the characters until I get what I want.

That love. That all-consuming, overwhelming, never-ending love is what I want. I want to feel what Darcy and Elizabeth feel. I want to look into someone's eyes and know I'm looking at my happily ever after.

The door opens, and I keep reading, my eyes skittering across the page and drinking in every word.

The door is open. Okay. So this is gonna be kinda awkward if this isn't Aston. Damn, why didn't I think of this before?

I slowly raise my eyes over the top of the book. Aston clicks the door shut behind him, smirking at me with a cocked eyebrow.

"Not that I'm complaining, but is there any reason you're on my bed?" he asks smoothly.

"I'm reading," I reply, dropping my gaze to the page again. "And I need to be comfy when I read, which will explain why I'm on your bed opposed to that horrible chair at the desk."

"I can see you're reading, Megs, but why are you reading in my room and not yours?"

"I can go if you'd like me to." I dog-ear the page and tuck the book under my arm.

"Hey, no! No, I didn't say that." He drops his bag and walks toward the bed, putting his hands either side of me. "I didn't even fucking think it."

"Oh. Well." I smile sweetly. "I'll just get back to my book, then."

"Hell fucking no," he mutters, grabbing the battered

book and dropping it on the floor. My mouth drops open.

"You did not just throw my book on the floor."

"I dropped it."

"No. You threw it. I should bitch slap you for hurting Mr. Darcy that way."

"Right. Because Mr. Darcy and his pompous ass will appreciate it."

I narrow my eyes a little, half-surprised he even knows who Mr. Darcy is. But then again, I'm quickly finding out that Aston isn't what he seems, and I like it. There's a whole other side to him I'm quickly coming to adore.

"You don't throw my books. Ever," I tell him firmly. His lips twitch. "I mean it. Next time you throw one of my babies, especially a favorite, I *will* hurt you."

He schools his face into a serious expression and climbs onto the bed, kneeling in front of me. "I'm sorry, baby," he murmurs, cupping the side of my face. "I won't throw one of your books ever again."

I smile at him, turning my cheek into his palm. "You damn well better not."

Aston touches his lips to mine and slides his hand round to the back of my head. He lowers me back on the bed slowly, his mouth moving against mine tenderly.

"I just realized that Braden is in classes all day. Which means I have you all to myself for a while." His lips travel along my jaw. "So there's no damn way you're reading a fucking book when you could be doing this." He runs a hand down my side and slips it under my shirt, his hand rough against my skin.

I arch my back into him slightly, my hands easing their way up his arms to his shoulders and neck as his lips find their way to mine. The hairs at the nape of his neck tickle. I curl my fingers around them, holding him against me. My leg bends and my foot travels up the back of his calf, his jeans rough against my bare toes.

His tongue explores my mouth, diving in and out, swirling in the same way desire is in my lower stomach. His probing hand below my top does nothing but ignite the fire inside me. It does nothing but continue to feed and fuel the storm of feelings I have whenever he's near me.

Aston trails his lips along my jaw to my ear, letting them fall away from my skin and resting his head next to mine. His breathing is heavy and full of pain.

"I still don't understand why you're here," he whispers.

"I'm here because I want to be." I trail a hand down his back, rubbing in slow, circular motions, and I know the demons inside him are rising up. The demons that keep him from me completely.

"But I don't understand why."

"Not everything needs an explanation. This is one of those things."

"What if a part of me needs one?" He pulls back, releasing me and kneeling up again.

I sit and cross my legs. My eyes find his, and I'm lost in the swirling torment that's in the shadows of them. His emotions are all battling each other with the force of a tornado – the color of his eyes darkened to the shade of a storm's heart. I'm aching to reach out and touch him but something tells me not to. Despite the lingering temptation tingling my fingers, I know I have to do this on his terms. I'm so angry at him and I don't even know why. I'm so confused about everything. I want to understand. I want to know what he keeps so buried down inside him, and I want to make it better.

"Then that's something I'll never be able to give you," I say quietly, sadly.

"Why?"

"Because my reasons for being here – the way I feel inside, what I feel about you, about us, about all of this – I can't put them into words. I could sit here for hours and try to explain, but I can't. They just … are."

He stands and turns away from me. He pulls his shirt over his head and tosses it into the corner of his room carelessly, the muscles in his back and arms flexing as he runs his hands through his hair.

"Aston. Talk to me," I say softly.

"Why? What difference would it make?"

"Because I need to understand! I need to understand you – all the difference faces of you. I know three. I know the guy, I know the lover, and I know whatever side of you this is, but I don't fucking understand them!" I stand. "One minute you're climbing through my bedroom window, then you're kissing me, then you're walking away from me. I don't get it!"

"Some things can't be explained," he says tightly,

throwing my own words back at me.

"Bullshit! *Bull. Shit*. Aston!" I walk toward his turned back. "Absolute crap! The way you act the way you do, the way you hide a part of yourself from everyone, all that has an explanation, it could be explained! You just choose not to. For some reason, you don't."

"Maybe I can't!" He turns to me, his eyes raw and his body taut. "Maybe I can't explain it all. Maybe I can't. Maybe it hurts too much. Did you ever think of that?"

His eyes drop, and I want to kick myself. I never thought of that. I never thought whatever it is he's keeping inside that haunts him so much is too painful for him to talk about. This whole time I've been thinking about how I feel about what he's going through. I've been so occupied with what his secrecy is doing to me, I haven't stopped to consider what it's doing to him. I haven't thought for one second about how he feels. God.

My hands reach out for him, and he grips my wrists in a lightning fast movement. "Don't," he whispers, his face hard. "Don't."

A minute passes between us, stretching out for an infinite amount of time. Neither of us move, the only sound between us the heaviness of his breathing, until he looks at me slowly. His eyes are filled with sadness, and I've never seen him look so vulnerable. I want to shake his hands off my wrists and touch him, soothe that pain, but I can't. I've tried.

Whatever he's going through he has to share for both of us. I can't think about me or him as separate people.

When it comes to the pain shining in his eyes, something has to give, because I need to know why, because the game isn't between us. The game is the show we put on for everyone around us. There's no charade when we're standing face to face like we are now. There's no charade when everything we feel is so, so real.

"You're so desperate to keep hold of me, yet you're so determined to keep me at arm's length," I whisper. "Why? Why can't you talk to me? What are you scared of?"

"I'm scared of keeping you and I'm scared of losing you. My whole life I've looked after myself, depended on myself, and I've kept everything at bay. All the feelings, everything. And then … Then I met you and everything changed. Everything I thought was real turned out to be a load of bullshit. The only thing that's real is you."

"Why me? Why do I make such a difference?"

He exhales slowly, resting his forehead against mine, his eyes burning into me. "Because I've *never* needed anyone as much as I need you. If I let you in, if I tell you everything, then you might not need me, too – and that is the fucking scariest thing of all. As much as I wish you'd walk away, as much as you should walk away, I don't think I'll ever be able to let you."

"Why would I go?" I frown.

He sighs, finally releasing my wrists and linking our fingers. "Because my past is different to yours, Megan. We come from two different places. We have two completely different stories–"

I shake my head. "You really believe that shit? Do

you?"

He doesn't move.

"You think your past will change the way I think about you? The way I feel? Because it won't. It won't change a goddamn thing!"

"Megan–"

I shake my head again, snatch my hands from his, and shove him away. I lean against the window and look out between the gaps in the curtains. "I'm not gonna walk away, Aston. I couldn't even if I wanted to. I'm in too far already. Whatever it is that's inside you and that's eating away at you … I want to *know*. I need to know for *us*."

I hear his steps as he crosses the room and feel the warmth of his body as he presses against my back. He rests his hands on my hips. They slowly creep round to my stomach, flattening out, and he buries his face in the side of my hair. I lean back into him, struggling with the rollercoaster of emotions running through my body.

"We're different, Megs," he whispers. "Too different. Even now we have to hide this."

"We only have to hide it because Braden will kick our asses, but we can't hide it forever."

"I don't want to hide this. I don't wanna hide you. Every guy that looks at you … I hate it. I hate the way they look at you like they just wanna fuck your brains out. It drives me fucking insane."

"The way you used to look at me, you mean?" I tease, smiling a little.

He laughs hollowly, turning me around. I wrap my

arms around his waist and lay my head against his bare chest. I listen to the beating of his heart, harsh and frantic.

"Yeah, the way I used to look at you until I did sleep with you. Fuck, Megs, when I kissed you I realized that wasn't all I wanted from you. It wasn't all I needed from you." His voice rumbles in his chest and he presses his lips to the top of my head.

"Then let me be what you need," I beg. "Don't think about Braden, or keeping this a secret, or where we come from. All that matters is we're here now and I'm here now. Let me be what you need me to be. Stop pushing me away, Aston, 'cause even though I should let it go I can't. I'll always come back."

His chest heaves with the force of his breath. "I will. I'll tell you everything. But not today, Megs. Soon. But not today."

I shut my eyes briefly. "You promise?"

Aston slides a hand up my back, over my shoulder, and cups my chin. He raises my face slightly, bending his down, and I meet his gray eyes. "I promise."

~

This is a mess.

I smile politely at the guy across the table from me. Date two on Lila's "Operation Get Megan a Boyfriend" and it's no better than the first. If I'm honest, it's even worse.

And it's not even the guy. No, Callum is lovely. He's sweet, he's hot, and he's funny. He's pretty much the perfect guy – but he's just not *my* perfect guy.

"Lila said you were an English major?" he asks, dipping his spoon into his ice-cream.

"Yeah. I've always loved literature so it makes sense to major in it."

"What do you plan to do when you graduate? I know it's a while away." His lips quirk up to the side. "But it's good to have a plan, you know?"

"Oh – I think I'll probably end up teaching it." I shrug. "Maybe I'll go into publishing, I'm undecided exactly what. I'd like to write a book one day though. What about you?"

"I hope to get into Harvard Med. It's not easy to do but I'm on the right track."

Well done, Lila. Not only do you set me up with a junior, you pick the one that's planning on going to the opposite side of the country in eighteen months.

"Wow. Quite the goal." I smile.

"Hey – yours isn't bad. At least you get to do what you love. My career choice is largely influenced by my family."

"Oh." Awkward. "It can't be that bad, right? Or you wouldn't do it?"

"No, it's my second choice career, so it's not hard."

"What was your first?" Oh, God. Am I acting too interested? I don't want to be rude but I don't want him to think I'm interested. Dammit. This whole thing is one giant clusterfuck.

Aston walks past the window and double-takes. My

eyes flick toward him, and I'm aware of Callum talking but I can't really hear him. I'm too focused on the clenching of Aston's fists and tightening of his jaw. He's pissed off.

Really pissed off.

"Megan?" Callum waves a hand in front of my face and I look back at him.

"I'm sorry – I just saw a friend I've been trying to call. It's kind of important." I inwardly flinch at my own lie. "Do you mind if I run after him?"

"Um, sure. Not at all."

"I'm so sorry." I get up from the table and put a bill down. "Here – toward lunch. I'm sorry."

I run out of the diner and after Aston, turning the same corner he did to leave the downtown area. I get to the end of the street and sigh. I can't see him or his car – and I have no idea when I'll get a chance to explain why he saw me having lunch with some other guy.

Damn Lila and Maddie and their stupid ideas!

I turn. Since I bailed on Callum heading back to campus is my best decision. And texting Aston would probably be a good idea. Damn secrecy.

I'm pulled down an alley and my back presses against cold bricks. Can't move – someone's heavy weight holds me back. Gray eyes capture mine before panic sets in.

"Do you make it a habit of sneaking up on girls?" I mutter.

"Only you," he responds. "But I'll be honest – I wasn't expecting to come downtown and find you having fucking lunch with another goddamn guy."

"Aston–"

"I'd be lying if I said I wasn't pissed, but then we're not exactly exclusive so I guess–"

"Lila set it up," I blurt out, silencing him. "She's going all Austen's *Emma* on me. She has this crazy idea that I need a boyfriend and is setting me up with guys she thinks Braden will be okay with. I can't refuse or she'll know something is up. I just turn up, talk, and that's it. I don't even give them my number. It's all fake."

"Fake?"

"Uh-huh. I just go so she doesn't get on my case about it. Besides, if it was a real date I wouldn't have left him there to come running here after you, would I?"

His body relaxes, tightness leaving his muscles, and he pulls me from the wall into his body. He presses my face into his neck. The way his arm is wound tightly around my body lets me know he wasn't lying when he said he didn't want to lose me.

And this wasn't anger. This was fear – of that exact thing happening.

I wrap my arms around his waist, holding him tightly.

"I don't know why I thought . . ." he trails off. "I'm such a fucking dick. I'm sorry, Megs."

"It's okay." I kiss his neck softly. "I probably would have thought the same if it was the other way around."

"No, baby, it's not fucking okay. I can't accuse you of that shit just because of my own issues–"

"You didn't accuse me of anything." I pull back, looking into his eyes. "If it was the other way around, I probably would have gone in there and ripped out her extensions."

He smirks. "I don't know how I didn't go in there and knock him out."

I run my fingertips across his back. "I don't know how you did it either. I hate even seeing other girls look at you," I say quietly.

"If Braden was anyone other than my best friend . . ." He shakes his head. "I'd tell him, but it ain't that damn easy." He sighs heavily. "I guess we're just gonna have to deal with Lila's bullshit plan and get on with it."

"But what if it's obvious? That there's a bigger reason I'm turning them down?"

"Then we cross that bridge together when we get there."

"There's only so many guys that can't be my type."

"Listen here." He turns my face so it's against his, our noses brushing. "There's only one fucking guy you need to worry about being your type, so every other dick can take a running jump off a cliff. In case you need reminding of that, baby, here's your reminder."

His lips crash into mine, his tongue forcing its way into my mouth possessively. He runs it along the length of mine forcefully, his hands pulling me ever closer to him. My own slide up his back, gripping onto his shoulders, and I let him claim me. I know this is what he needs, and the deepness of his kiss that tugs on my lower stomach muscles proves me right.

"I think I'm good on the reminder," I whisper as he pulls away, pressing our cheeks together. "But any time you feel the need to remind me fully ..."

His fingers dig into my back. "Any time I feel the need to remind you fully ..." He turns his face, his lips barely touching my ear. "It'll be a reminder you'll never fucking forget."

Chapter Fourteen - Aston

Seeing her with another guy – no matter how innocent or friendly it was – put a part of my brain into overdrive that's only ever roared to life for me. The need to grab her arm, drag her out of that diner, and pin her against the wall while I kissed her senseless almost took over. The need to protect her from every other ass in this town, hell, in the state, was almost our undoing.

It's something no one would understand. For the first time in my life I've started to let someone in, let them *be* there, all while taking what they have to offer. And that's the problem. I'm taking from Megs but I'm not giving back to her – I'm not giving her what she deserves, yet, somehow, she knows exactly what I seem to need. All the time.

For the first time in my life I've let myself feel something other than the things that fuck up my mind. I've let her in. The one girl I knew could undo me with a simple smile or one glance into those little blue eyes – and she does. Every single time, she undoes me like she's tugging on a loose string of a hand-knitted blanket, and all I can do is unravel in front of her.

The craziest thing is that I want to unravel. I want to tell her everything she wants to know. I want to tell her why I'm a fucked up mix of hot and cold toward her, why I pull her into me and then push her away. But telling her

… Telling her might just push it over the edge.

Telling her could push her away and make me permanently cold.

Telling her would mean accepting. Reliving. Remembering. *Feeling.*

Apart from Gramps, she is the only person I've ever felt something for. She's the only person I've wanted to feel for, and what I feel is spiraling out of my control. It's growing along with my need for her, which is way stronger than it should be, way more addicting than it should be.

Because that's what she is. She's addicting. The vanilla smell of her hair, the light in her eyes, the brightness of her smile, the soft skin of her hand; every part of her is addicting to me.

And even more than that … She sees me. She doesn't see the jackass who fucks everything with a pulse, or the cocky, arrogant bastard who cares about no one other than himself. Or maybe she does see that – she just sees what's under it, too. She sees the real me, the one that no one else ever bothered to see.

She sees the broken. She sees the mismatched. She sees the fucked up.

And pretty soon, she's gonna grab hold of that fucked up and pull it out of me in a gut wrenching conversation.

~

"It's not working," Megan's voice echoes down the

hall. "Make her stop with her stupid dates."

"There's nothing I can do," Maddie replies. "You know what she's like. She thinks she's damn cupid or something."

"One success – a third of success – with you and Braden doesn't make her cupid! It doesn't make me cupid, either. Shit. Has she ever thought maybe I'm happy as I am?"

"You'll have to ask her. I just yes or no to the guys, Megs. Seriously, you should see some of the dicks she had lined up. It would have been like walking into a strip club – just without the sexy."

"Ughghghghgh." Megan bangs her head on the table as I walk into the kitchen, grinning.

"What's up? Being forced on dates such a hard life?" I smirk as she lifts her head.

"How would you know?" she throws back at me. "I wasn't even aware you got your 'date's' name before you ripped her panties off her."

"Touché," Maddie mutters.

"Oh, I do, sometimes. But that's usually all I get." I shrug and lean against the counter. "Better to be nameless and get fucked than forced onto dates with a bunch of pretty boys."

"Oh, because you're not counted in the pretty boy category? How long did it take you to do your hair this morning?" She raises an eyebrow. "Probably longer than it took half my dorm combined, Mr. Maybelline."

"I could probably make you come quicker than I

could do my hair," I respond, watching her cheeks flush slightly. "But that doesn't mean I'm a fucking pretty boy."

"Let me guess – it makes you a sexy boy?"

I grin. "I'm glad you think so."

"I never said I thought so, asshole. It was a question, not a statement. Still learning the difference?"

I move to the table, leaning across it toward her. "No, but with your sass, it looks like you could do with a lesson learning the difference between a slapped ass and a spanked ass. Want a teacher, Megs?"

Her mouth drops open, and I fight the urge to lean even closer to her and make her close it. I see Maddie smirk, amused, out the corner of my eye, and let my own lips curve into a smirk.

"If I ever feel the need to be taught a slightly kinky side of sex," Megan says in a lower voice and leans forward slightly, pushing her boobs together. She's pushing this right to the fucking limit. "Then I'd find a teacher who could play my body like a guitar, strumming all the right strings at the right times, not a horny college boy just looking to get off."

"How do you know I'm not the guitar player?"

"How do you know you are?" she challenges, sitting back and letting her mouth curve upwards.

"It takes me ten minutes to do my hair. I could make you come in half that," I threaten and promise her, my eyes still fixed on hers. "If you can find a damn guitar player that can do that, then I'll salute you, Miss Harper. Until then, you can imagine *my* fingers plucking your body like the strings of a guitar."

I scoop an apple up from the bowl in between us and take a bite, winking at her as I leave the kitchen.

"Pig!" she yells after me. I hear Maddie's quiet laughter, and grin to myself. Sometimes, being known as an asshole who likes to get into girls' pants is a good thing – and in a situation like that when she's turning me the fuck on, it's definitely a good thing.

I rest against the wall outside the frat house, finish the apple, and throw the core in the bin. I spy Braden stretching round the side of the house and jog over to him.

"Ready to run?"

He looks up, grabbing two water bottles. "I thought your lazy ass was still in bed."

"Yeah it was, but pissing Megan off was so much more fun." I shrug, grin, and take off with him behind me.

"I dunno why you do it, man. One of these days she will hand your balls to you." He shakes his head.

"She's too irrational for that. She gets pissed off way too easily to even consider ripping my balls off."

"Yeah – but you've heard Kay's revenge methods, right? I heard her last week seething to Maddie that she wanted to 'take a butter knife to the underside of that fucking asshat's balls and put them on the school menu as a special with a side of fish to represent the whore he thought he could fuck right before her.'" He takes a deep breath, and I flinch a little.

"Ouch. Who pissed her off?"

"Dude, I don't know, and I don't think I fucking

want to."

"Wait," I muse. "I thought she was a lesbian?"

"Bisexual," he corrects me. "She likes both."

"Oh, man. So none of us are safe from her loud-mouth ass?" I shake my head. "Damn."

"Right?" he agrees. "So, me and the guys were thinking of heading into San Francisco tomorrow night for the weekend. Maddie and Lila are coming – not sure about Megan, though."

My muscles instantly tighten, my stomach clenching at the mention of my home city. It's so close to Berkeley, yet so far away. The six year old Aston that left San Francisco is a completely different person to the nineteen year old Aston living in Berkeley, but that doesn't mean it's a place I can even consider going.

"Don't think so," I reply, trying to keep my shaking voice even. "I gotta see my Gramps on Sunday. Old coot nearly whacked me with his fucking stick for not showing up that weekend we went to Vegas."

Braden laughs, taking me at my – very true – word. "Alright, alright. You stay back here like a good little dickhead and fuck some other poor girl."

"That's the plan."

Or it's not. But he doesn't need to know the real one.

We stop for a second to drink and catch our breath, and I take my cell from my pocket.

Are you going to SF? I send to Megan.

She replies instantly. *I don't know. Are you?*

No. Don't go.

Okay. I won't.

I slip it back into my pocket, looking up into Braden's curious face. "What?"

"I don't think I've ever seen you text anyone. Girl finally get your number out of you?"

I snort. "Don't be so fucking stupid. If I did that I'd never get any damn peace between them and you and Ryan."

"True that." Braden nods, and we start running back in the direction of the frat house to get ready for class.

We change quickly, meeting back outside to head into the main building for English. Maddie and Megan are waiting for us when we get downstairs, and Megan's tapping her foot impatiently.

"Are you girls ready? Some of us actually want to pass this year," she says sarcastically.

"Oh, Meggy," Braden mutters, taking Maddie's hand. "You could pass this class in a fucking coma. You've probably read everything on the semester plan already."

She slaps the back of his head, and he curses.

"The fuck was that for?"

Maddie slaps his chest with her books. "Language!"

"You sound like my mom," he mutters.

Megan grins at Maddie, her eyes flicking to Braden. "Just because you're right about the reading thing doesn't mean I have to like it. Maybe if you paid a bit more attention to the class you'd pass without looking over my shoulder when we have work due in."

"Why did I never think of that?" I look at Braden.

"Because you're apparently a fucking genius in your own right," he grumbles. "Am I the only stupid one here?"

"Oh, you're not stupid," Maddie soothes him. "You're just a little bit slower than us."

"You know what, Angel? It's a really good job I love you."

"I think so, too." She smiles. "It means I can say exactly what everyone else is thinking."

He gives her a look that says she'll get it later, and she smiles wider.

"Hold up," Megan pauses, staring at Braden. "Did you just call *Aston* a genius?"

"I did."

"They're not words I'd ever expect to hear in the same sentence."

"Fuck off." I tug on her hair, and she swats at me.

"I'm not jokin', Meggy. This kid graduated with a fucking 3.8 GPA."

Megan looks at me now, her eyebrows raised and surprise in her eyes. "You did?"

I shrug. "One of us assholes has to be smart."

"No, really? You did?"

She's not acting here. She's genuinely surprised, and I don't know whether or not to be pissed she doesn't believe me. "Yeah."

"I can't believe you have the same GPA as me. You don't look that smart." She smirks wickedly, and I know the smile is for Braden and Maddie's benefit.

I hold the class door open for her, looking down as she pauses in front of me, and my hand brushes her hip. "Not everyone is what they seem, Megan. You should know that by now."

She looks up at me, her startling blue eyes full of questions I know I have to answer.

"I know that. I just wish those people could trust in the people that care a little." She sweeps past me to our desk. I bite the inside of my lip and follow after her.

"Maybe it's not that they don't trust," I say. "Maybe it's that they've forgotten how to."

She straightens her books on the desk, slowly turning her face to me as I sit next to her. "Then maybe they should open their eyes and see that the person they need to trust is right in front of them. Maybe they should open up and share so they don't have to bear the burden alone."

"Not everything is made to be shared. Not every scar is on the body. Some scars are on the mind. Some scars can't be seen. They're inside, burned in so deeply that they'll never be healed."

Her eyes are earnest and soft. "Just because a scar can't be healed doesn't mean it can't be soothed," she whispers.

Fuck. She's so right, and this weekend is the perfect time with everyone gone. But am I ready? I don't know. I don't know if I'll ever be ready to talk about my childhood, but I don't have a choice if I want to keep her. If I want to keep this girl in my arms, secret relationship be fucking damned, I have to be honest with her.

I take a deep breath and make a decision I know I'll regret. A decision that will change everything.

A decision that will change me.

"Sometimes the dark truth is too much for some people," I warn her.

A decision that will change her.

"Sometimes a light dusting of the truth isn't enough," she responds.

A decision that will change us.

"Is the dark really better than the light?"

She nods. "Sometimes. Sometimes you need to get lost in the dark to truly appreciate the light."

"This weekend," I drop my voice so it's barely audible. "I can't promise everything. I can only promise what is there to give."

She blinks once, her hand twitching. She clenches her fist and puts it in her lap. "I've only ever had half of you. I'm sure I can wait a little longer for all of you."

~

A night of fitful sleep, recurring nightmares and horror flashbacks aren't how I wanted to start my day. Now, with the guys off to SF, Megan can get in and out of the house fairly unbothered. If anyone asks, she has a spare key to Braden's room and left some books there. If anyone asks why she's in my room, I borrowed one of the books. It's hardly foolproof, but then again, no one here will care that much.

They all secretly want in her pants.

"You really wanna know?" I look at her across the room.

Her light blue eyes are wide and earnest as she meets my weary gaze. She pulls her knees to her chest and bites her thumbnail, nodding slowly. I sink onto the bed opposite her, the springs creaking under the heaviness of my body, and gaze out of the window.

"It's not an easy thing to listen to," I warn her.

"I want to be there for you," she replies softly, shifting a little closer to me. "But I can't be there if I don't understand, not really. And I want to, Aston – I want to understand. I want to know all of you."

I take a deep breath. It doesn't matter if I'm ready or not anymore – it's too late to back out. I have to tell her everything, tell her things I've never said out loud before. And somehow, when I look into her eyes, I find the strength within me to say the words.

"I have no idea who my father is. My mom got herself knocked up at seventeen to a guy whose name she didn't even know." My voice is hard, bitterness coating every word thickly. "She palmed me off on my Gramps whenever she could; she wasn't cut out to be a mom – at least at seventeen. Gramps insists she suffered from post-partum depression, but she didn't care. Not really. If she did, she would have seen a doctor instead of medicating herself with alcohol and the cheapest drug she could get ahold of.

"CPS kept in contact with us until I was sixteen and

considered 'stable' by them. I stole my file once and read it. It says that 'Mom' moved us into a stingy little apartment when I was two, and although there were complaints from neighbors about hearing a child screaming and being left alone, whenever they visited everything was perfect. I was clean, the apartment was clean, and she was clean. They couldn't do anything without proof." The view from my room is a far cry from the dirty alleys of the Tenderloin district in San Francisco. "Despite the area we lived in she always managed to make it seem like we lived somewhere else whenever they showed up.

"I didn't need to read the report much further. I have memories from when I was about four, spanning the next two years. 'Stepdads' that came and went repeatedly. All the same. All big, tattooed, and more stuck on drugs and alcohol than even she was. They all hated me with a passion."

Dirty little son of a bitch. Fuckin' runt. You piece of shit.

"They showed it whenever she went out to earn money – when she went to sell her body to some rich prick to fund the drug habit for herself and whichever poor bastard she was fucking at the time. That's when it would start."

"Mommy," I had whimpered, cowering in the corner of the kitchen and hugging the smelly rabbit to my body. He leaned over me – I didn't know his name. I never

knew their names. They were never there long enough for me to know them.

"Your mommy can't hear you," he mocked. "She's busy being a whore to get me the good shit. She's good at that."

"I want my mommy." I pushed back further into the corner, the cable jack cutting into the bare skin on my back. Tears formed in my eyes and I curled up tighter, scared of the big man in front of me. The smell of alcohol on his breath fell over me and I covered my nose and hid my face.

It was pointless. I knew, even then, that he wouldn't touch my face. They never did.

"Face hits were too obvious. A bruise on the back? On the legs? Even the stomach. They were safer for them. They weren't questioned, and when they were, it was the same answer."

"Oh, that?" Mom had gently stroked my back, her eyes steady on the social worker's. "We went to the park a few days ago and the silly boy thought he could swing off the big monkey bars. I turned away for a second – a friend called me over – then he was on his back on the floor. He's got no sense of danger. I've tried to explain, but he is only four. We came home and cleaned it up good, though. Didn't we, little dude?"

Her blue-gray eyes found mine, a spark of fear in them. I nodded.

"Mommy made it all better."

"I fell off the table. I tripped on a crack on the sidewalk. I slipped on the stairs outside the apartment. There was always an excuse. Never a hospital visit. Always my fault. Never theirs."

The glass had hit the wall hard enough that it shattered. I screamed, slipping on a wet patch on the floor as I tried to escape to my room for an extra second of relief. I fell to my knees, fear pulsing through my body. I sobbed, cried, whimpered. I gulped desperately at air, my throat tight. I pulled myself along the floor, scrambling to escape the angry shadow approaching me.

The glass cut right through my palm, and I screamed again. Blood mixed with the clear alcohol on the floor, swirling in patterns, and someone banged on the door.

"Fucking nosey bastards," the man grumbled, picking me up. I fought against his hold, and he lowered his mouth to my ear. "Don't fuckin' fight me, rat, or you'll have my belt across your back." I stilled. "Good boy."

The door opened and the old woman across the hall was there with a worried look. "I heard a smash and a scream – is everything okay?"

"Fine. The boy knocked my glass off the side while I wasn't in the room and tried cleaning it up – cut his hand a couple times. If you don't mind, I need to clean him up." He shut the door on his lies.

"Every time. She knew. She never cared enough. All she cared about was sticking another ounce of shit into her bloodstream or snorting another gram. All she gave a fuck about was the bottom of her glass."

One day, maybe you'll be useful and we can send you out to earn the money instead of your whore of a mother.

A fist. Another bruise.

That's all she's good for. Fucking. It's all you'll be good for one day.

A kick to the back.

No-one is ever gonna want you. Not when they find out how much of a fucking slut your mother is.

A bang of the head on a chair leg.

You're only good for what she is. No-one will ever care about you.

"Stop," a soft, pained voice whispers. Hands press tenderly against my cheeks, lips brush my forehead. "You can stop now."

I open my eyes that must have closed while I was lost in my head. Megan's blue eyes are brimming with tears.

"You can stop," she repeats. "You're safe here. You're safe with me." She strokes my cheek as a tear rolls down hers. "You're safe."

The fog begins to clear, the memories pushing back, and I see her clearly. The pain etched on her face is something I never want to see again. It's something I put there. This is why I never wanted to tell her. This is why I never wanted to get this close to her.

"Don't cry for me, baby." I brush my thumb under her eye. "I'm not worth your tears."

She nods. "You are. You're worth every last tear in my body."

"I'm not," I argue, moving away from her. I shove off the bed and begin to pace the floor, the old words reopening the scars and reinforcing everything I've tried to push back. Reminding me of what I am. Reminding me of the worth of my life, of my body. "I'm not worth you. Don't you get it? They were fucking right, Megs. I'm not worth anything. I'm too fucked up. Everything they ever said – every time they told me I wasn't worth shit, every time they told me no-one would ever want me–"

"They were wrong," she says in a small but strong voice. "They were *wrong*. All of it. It was all lies."

I press my hands against the wall and clench my jaw. "Nah. They were right. Every fucking one of them. I'm fucked up. I'm broken, a bunch of mismatched pieces stuck together in a shit attempt at being fixed."

The bed springs squeak and the floorboards creak. A soft hand touches my back, another wraps around my tightened bicep.

"They weren't right. They were far from being right."

"You don't know that."

"Yes I do." She wraps her hands around my arm and rests her head against me. She tightens her grip, resting the side of her face against my shoulder. "They were wrong, because I want you. I want all of you – even the broken parts and the mismatched parts."

I find her eyes. "Why? Why? I can't give you what you really want. I can't give you sunshine and fucking rainbows. I can't give you puppies and fluffy bunnies. I can't give you the perfect you deserve."

"I don't want perfect, and if I want sunshine and rainbows, I'll go to the local elementary school and visit the kindergarten class."

I push off from the wall, her hands falling away. "It'll always end up as sex. There's nothing inside, baby. I'm fucking empty."

"You're lying and you know it."

"Am I?" I turn, pinning her with my gaze. I am lying – but it's better this way. "Am I lying? You think I feel anything when I take some girl back on a Saturday night? You think I feel anything other than sex?"

Silence stretches, and I fucking hate myself for this. I hate myself for pushing away the one person I want to pull into me.

"I know you don't feel anything other than sex when you take a girl back to your room on a Saturday night."

That's more painful than the physical kicks to the stomach I used to get. "So why are you still here?"

"Because I'm not just any girl," she says with

certainty, her eyes boring into mine. "Do you think I'm dumb, Aston? You just bared your soul to me – the deepest, darkest parts of it – and now you're trying to push me away. Who are you really trying to protect, huh? Is it me or is it you? Do you feel nothing for me when you call me 'baby'? Do you feel nothing when you hold me against you? Do you honestly feel nothing when we're together? Go on. Tell me! Tell me that right now, with me looking into your eyes that you feel nothing, and I'll walk out that damn door. Tell me you don't care."

I can't.

"Tell me!"

And she knows it.

"Go on!"

"I can't!" I yell. "I can't fucking tell you that! And that's the problem. You have to go. You have to walk away, because I can't. You have to protect yourself from me, because I can't walk away from you."

"I don't want you to!" She storms across the room. "I don't want you to walk away from me!" She stops in front of me, her chest heaving, and continues in a quieter voice, "I don't want you to walk away."

No one will ever want you. No one will care. You're not worth shit. Son of a bitch. Useless prick.

I grab her and pull her against me, burying my face in her hair. I'm shaking as I hold her. I need her – I don't know what it is, but I need her more than I've ever needed anything. She's all I can feel. She makes me want to rip apart the mismatched pieces of myself and put them back in the right places. She awakens something in me, a will to live, a will to *love.* With her arms wrapped around my waist, her hands spread against my back, and her head tucked into my neck, it feels like home.

Megan feels like home to me.

Chapter Fifteen - Megan

"Did she really never tell you about your dad?" I ask, drawing circles on Aston's arm with my fingertip.

"No. Gramps told me a few years ago she went away for a friend's birthday and a few weeks later found out she was pregnant. She swore there was only him but she couldn't remember his name," he replies. "It doesn't matter, anyway. I have my Gramps, and that's what matters. He was there when no one else was."

"He sounds like an amazing man," I say, tilting my head back and staring into his gray eyes. "It makes it easy to understand where you get it from."

He makes a noise of disbelief. "I'm not amazing, baby, far from it."

"The beauty of being an outsider is that I can see what you can't," I argue. "You might not see it yet, you might never see it, but you are." I raise my hand to his face, stroke my thumb down his cheek and across the faint stubble on his jaw. And I'm not lying – I can see everything he can't. I can see the beauty of him hiding behind the ugly memories of his past. He just needs to let it shine through.

"If you say so." He catches my hand in his and kisses each of my fingers softly.

"I'm sorry I made you remember those things," I say in a small voice.

"I'm not," he replies firmly. "I'm not sorry you did.

You were right yesterday. You have to get lost in the dark to appreciate the light. My head is full of darkness, full of shadows and horrors, and then I look into your eyes. It's like finding the light at the end of the tunnel – the light I never thought I'd find."

I flatten my hand against his cheek, his resting atop mine, and move my face forward so our lips brush. "I like that. I love that I make you feel that way."

"It's true. Who else could I threaten about spanking across the kitchen table?" His lips twitch, a bit of the normal light returning to his eyes as the darkness recedes.

"I'm sure you could find someone." I shrug a shoulder.

"I probably could, but I don't want to find someone." His face turns serious again, and his hand trails along my arm and rests on my back. "I have to tell you something else – but you have to promise me you won't get mad and leave."

"I'm. Not. Leaving." I put extra emphasis on each word. "Okay? I'm not going anywhere."

For a second I see a glimpse of the little boy he keeps inside flash in his eyes, and my heart breaks a little. A tiny crack forms for the pain he must feel.

"A few nights ago I went to this bar. It's out the way, and I went there because I had to prove to myself I'm not like my mom was." He closes his eyes, gathers himself, and opens them again. "I knew if I went in there and left with someone, I'd be no better than she was."

I swallow, trying not to let my facial expression

change as a little bile rises up my throat. Even as my whole body tightens, a part of me believes he didn't. He's stronger than that. A part of me has to believe that.

"And?"

Outside my voice is calm, deceptively so, but inside my body is raging. It's raging that he'd try it, raging at the people who made him this way, raging at the words he must have heard so many times to make him believe he's no better than his mom.

"I couldn't. I was in there for maybe five minutes, tops, and I had to leave. I had to run. It wasn't me." He looks steadily into my eyes. "And you're the reason I left. Hell, you're the reason I went. I told myself that if I went and left alone, I was good enough for you. If I left alone, I cared, I had feelings. If I left alone, I wasn't hollow inside."

"You're not hollow inside." I prop myself up on my elbow and look down at him, running my fingers through his hair. "You do feel – you must have felt to go in the first place. And as for being good enough for me ..." I shake my head. "Who dictates that? Society? A TV show? A romance novel? No. Not even Braden can dictate that, Aston. The only person who decides if someone is good enough for me, is me, and I say you are most definitely good enough for me."

He tucks my hair behind my ear. "How do you know?"

I smile a little. "Well, you're no Mr. Darcy, but you know ..."

His fingers move against my side, tickling me, and I

fall backwards onto the bed, laughing. He leans over me, his leg slipping between mine and his hips pinning me down. His hand leaves my side and travels up my body to my hand where he links our fingers.

"'You have bewitched me, body and soul,'" he murmurs, looking down into my eyes. "I forgot the accent, but I'm sure that'll do. That's all I can remember of the book when I look at you."

"One of my favorite lines." I smile. "Do I make you forget things often?"

"All the time." He lowers his lips, moving them softly across mine for a long, lingering moment.

"I can't believe you actually know some Jane Austen," I muse, moving his hair from his face.

How many guys know Jane Austen? Every day he surprises me a little more.

"It was the first classic novel my Gramps made me read. I was eight." He props his head on his hand. "He said that although Darcy was a pompous ass in the beginning, if I grew up and loved a woman the way he loved Elizabeth in the end, then he'd done his job at raising me." He trails a finger down the side of my face.

"He gave you the book to teach you to respect women," I say in awe. "He wanted you to take Darcy's journey of respecting and loving Elizabeth and apply it to real life. Your Gramps is a genius."

"I'll tell him you said that." He grins.

"I'll tell him myself if I ever get to meet him."

"You can. If you want to."

"Really?"

Aston nods. "I've already told you the worst. Gramps … Well, he'll probably be happy to have someone to talk to who actually enjoys discussing literature's greatest love stories. Hell, I don't have much patience for that shit."

"I would love to meet him," I say honestly. "And discuss literature's greatest love stories."

"Tomorrow?" Aston questions, the little boy showing in his eyes again, and I realize he's letting me in.

By taking me to meet his Gramps, he's giving me more of himself. He's letting me meet the one person who really knows him … The one person that knows the little boy inside.

I run the pad of my thumb along his bottom lip. "Tomorrow. I'll be sure to bring Mr. Darcy."

"No need." He drops his face to mine again, taking my bottom lip between his and sucking lightly. "I'll be a real life Mr. Darcy."

"You don't have the top hat and tails," I protest, clasping my hands behind his head.

"Who needs them? They'd end up on the floor anyway."

I giggle as he kisses me again, his body pressing into mine. "You're probably right."

~

I feel like I'm fifteen and sneaking back into my room after breaking curfew.

I never intended to stay at the frat house last night – it just happened. After Aston told me everything, I couldn't leave. I couldn't walk away, leaving him with the memories I made him drag out.

So that's why I'm creeping out in yesterday's clothes to change quickly before he takes me to meet his Gramps.

Hoping everyone else is still in bed or doing what they normally do on a Sunday morning, I silently pad my way down the stairs. Kyle's deep voice makes me pause.

"A blonde girl?" he asks.

"Yeah. I didn't see who it was, though. As far as I know she was still in his room last night."

"You mean Aston didn't come down and pull some chick?"

Fuck.

I press my hand over my mouth to stifle the stream of curse words. I glance at the front door. If I turn the corner right now, whoever is outside will see me and know *I* was the girl in his room.

"Megan?" a voice asks, and I bite my tongue.

"Nah. Braden would kill him."

That's it.

I take my pumps off and skip up the stairs on tip toes. My hands shake as I fumble for Braden's key in the pocket of my jeans and slip it in the lock. I sneak into his room, and take one of my books from his desk.

Thank you, Braden, for your constant need to copy my English notes.

The door clicks shut behind me, and I put my pumps

back on. I know I look on the rough side of human – hey, it is a Saturday – but I walk casually down the stairs anyway. Kyle and the other guy, Mark, both look at me as I appear in their line of view.

"Morning." I smile and wave slightly.

"Uh," Kyle says awkwardly. "You're here early."

I lift the book. "Braden had my notes again. It's exactly why I have a key for his room."

"Seriously?" Mark narrows his eyes, looking at me suspiciously.

"The book is in my hand, isn't it? Want me to take you up and show you how many of my damn books he has sitting on his desk?" I offer, pointing to the stairs more calmly than I feel. "It's no big deal."

"Nah, you're alright," he replies, relaxing.

"Great." I fake a smile. "I'd love to stay and chat, but I have a paper to write. See ya."

"Bye, Megs." Kyle waves as I turn and leave the frat house.

All the air rushes from my lungs when the door shuts behind me, and I force myself to walk instead of run. *Shit.* That was close – too fucking close – and I've exhausted my number one excuse for being at the frat house when Braden or the girls aren't.

"Where the fuck were you last night?"

Kay's voice sends a bolt of panic through me. Hell. Can I get a break today?

"Why do you need to know?" I ask, letting myself into the dorm block.

"Because I came round here to bring your ass to a party – not with those dicks at Braden's house – and you weren't here. Where were you?"

I put my hand on my doorframe, grinning, and decide to play it coy. "Wouldn't you like to know?"

She smirks. "Fucking right I'd like to know. Did you finally get some?"

I shove the door open. "A lady never reveals her secrets!" And slam it shut before she can question me further.

"You bitch!" she yells, banging on the door. "I'm not letting this go!"

"I know!" But at least now I have time to come up with an excuse.

I exhale, a long, tortured sigh, and rest my forehead on the door. Who thought a secret relationship was a good idea?

Oh, yeah, me.

That was before the secret relationship became something complex, more than just a boy and a girl. Now it's entwined deeply in a past filled with horrors I can't even imagine, voices I'll never hear, and memories I'll never see fully. It's not just a passing college fling, something to pass the time.

It's real.

It's as real as a relationship could ever be.

I straighten and chuck the book on my bed, not caring when it slips to the floor, and strip as I head to the shower. A quick hot shower should sort me out and relax me from this morning's close calls. Too many in such a short space of time. There's only so many excuses I can come up with before the truth will have to come out, and I know that moment will be so explosive that even the Chinese New Year won't be able to touch it with their fireworks.

I step from the shower and run through the motions of getting ready, standing in front of my closet for longer than necessary. I mean, this is the equivalent of the "Meet the Parents" moment, right? So a good impression – literature aside – is necessary. But what the hell do you wear to meet someone's grandfather?

The gray sky outside makes me rethink my skirt idea. I pull out a pair of jeans instead and couple them with a colorful shirt and wrap-around sweater. I blast my hair with the hairdryer, clipping it away from my face with a flower pin, and smudge on some make up.

My cell buzzes and a message from Aston pops up. *Ready when you are.*

Give me five.

Convinced that it'll be sunny I grab a light jacket and sunglasses, and leave the dorm room. The sky has darkened only a little. It won't rain. Yet.

The walk downtown doesn't take long, and I find Aston parked exactly where he said he'd be. I knock on the window, smiling, and he leans over to open the door. I get in and he leans over the gearstick to kiss me soundly.

"Risky," I mutter.

"And being seen in a car with you isn't?" he shoots

back, amused.

I produce my glasses from under my jacket and slip them on. "See? I'm in disguise."

"You still look like you." He grins as he pulls out. "We're not passing campus, anyway. It's still early, so I doubt many people will be about."

"You say that. If I was Pinocchio, my nose would be about ten foot long I've told so many lies this morning."

"Who to?" He glances at me.

"Kyle and Mark, then Kay," I grumble. "Kyle and Mark think I'd slipped in to grab a book from Braden's room, and Kay thinks I was with a guy all night."

"Which is right. But she doesn't know?"

"No. She doesn't know. I slammed my door in her face."

"She won't let that go."

"I know. But I have time to make a decent excuse as to why I can't tell her who I was with."

He sighs. "You know she's gonna tell Lila and Maddie, and they'll be on your case, right?"

I tuck my hair behind my ear and chew on my thumbnail. "I know," I mumble. "But I didn't have to think. I was still reeling from Kyle and Mark. She caught me off-guard. I'm a real crappy secret girlfriend."

"I like that."

"That I'm a crappy secret girlfriend?" I frown at him as he pulls up outside a tidy, two-story house with perfectly pruned bushes and flowers.

"No, well, yeah." He turns, his gray eyes light and

piercing straight into mine. He smiles, grabbing my hand and tugging me toward him. "The girlfriend part."

I blush a little as I realize it's the first time either of us have said that word. "Oh, um . . ."

His lips touch mine, and he mutters against me, "Don't. I like the thought of you being my girlfriend, even if you are secret."

"Like Romeo and Juliet?"

"Save the literature for Gramps." He leans back and smiles. "But, yeah, kinda. Just without the dyin' and stuff."

I put my hand on the door handle and smile at him over my shoulder. "I can totally go for that."

My feet touch the ground and I realize how nervous I am. When it's me and Aston and we're messing around, talking, I don't feel nervous. But now I'm standing in front his Gramps' house, my heart is pounding and my palms are getting sweaty. I run my tongue over my lips, wetting them since they're suddenly dry, and swallow.

Aston takes my hand, linking our fingers, and pulls me toward the house. "Don't be scared."

"Does he know I'm here?"

He grins, his hand on the door handle. "Nope."

My mouth drops, and he pushes the door open, letting out the smell of cigar smoke.

"I wish you wouldn't smoke those damn things, Gramps!" he calls.

"So you keep sayin', boy, and I keep sayin' I ain't gonna stop."

Aston grins again, and I get the feeling this is a

routine for them. "Well if you're smokin' now, put the thing out. I brought company."

"Better not be one of those jackass frat boys you live with," his Gramps grumbles.

"No, it's not one of those jackasses." Aston chuckles slightly. "Better than that. Much better."

"What, you bring me a stripper?"

"Uh, no. Maybe next time."

I smile, loving the easy banter between the two.

"Well? Who is it?"

We step into the front room, and an old man is sitting quietly in an armchair at the far end of the room. He turns his head from where he was looking out the window, and I can see interest spark in his gray eyes. Gray eyes the exact same shade as Aston's.

"This is Megan," Aston introduces us. "Megan, this is my Gramps. Just call him Gramps."

"Hell, she's a pretty thing, ain't she, boy?" Gramps says, looking at me and smiling. "Come sit down, darlin', and don't you mind him. His manners are a bit iffy since he started hanging around with those jackass frat boys."

I laugh slightly and let Aston lead me over to the sofa opposite his Gramps. I sit on the cozy cushions, and Aston stops mid-sit.

"Let me guess. You want me to remember my manners and go get Megs a drink?" he asks with a raised eyebrow.

"Off you go."

I smile at Aston's exaggerated sigh, and I can almost

see the closeness in their relationship. It's not just the fact Aston is so alike his Gramps, just sixty or so years younger, it's in their easy banter and the affectionate smiles they have. His Gramps' comments remind me so much of my Nan – she's a crazy old thing with a penchant for "hot young things," as she puts it, but I love her.

Gramps looks at me and winks. "Gotta keep the boy on his toes. So, Megan, are you the girlfriend?" He looks so much like Aston in that second I can't help but smile wider.

"That's me."

"He never mentioned you before."

"It's, um … Complicated."

"Protective older brother ready to kick some pretty-boy ass?"

I think I love this man.

"Something like that." I grin. "Best friend."

"Jackass frat boy?" he questions.

I nod.

"See, boy? I told you they're all jackasses. Were in my day, still are now."

"And you raised the biggest one," Aston pats the old man's shoulder, putting a tray of drinks on the table and passing me one.

"Thank you." I look up at him, feeling a little shy now we're in front of his gramps.

"Damn right. And he's a pretty boy! No one can tell me I did half a job raisin' you, kid." Gramps grins, raises his glass of lemonade, and takes a drink before setting it back on the table. "So, Megan, do you like literature?"

Aston smirks, resting his arm on the sofa behind me, and I smile. "It's my major."

Gramps' eyes light up and he sits up a little straighter. "Favorite novelist?"

"Jane Austen. Pride and Prejudice, before you ask."

"By God, boy!" he exclaims in glee and claps his hands. "We have a keeper with this one!" He turns to me again. "Second favorite?"

I chew my lip for a second. "Dickens or Louisa May Alcott. It's tough, but Alcott might just win out. Her ability to create a whole cast of compelling, lovable characters – not just one or two – is something I've yet to find in another writer."

Gramps shakes his head. "You're telling me *Little Women* is better than *Great Expectations*?"

"Oh, no," I say. "Not better – the stories are on par with each other, but their styles are very different. My preference runs with Alcott's style, and I have a bit of a crush on Laurie." I shrug a shoulder.

"How many boys in books are you dating?" Aston pokes my shoulder. "First Darcy, now Laurie …"

"The proper term is book boyfriend," I correct him. "And there are many swoon-worthy characters in the literary world, new and old."

"What about if I was in a book?" He grins. "Would I be your book boyfriend?"

"God help the world if someone ever wrote you into a book, boy," Gramps grumbles. "That would be a literary disaster."

Aston sticks his tongue out, and Gramps laughs.

"Be nice, old man, or I'll hide the walking stick."

"Hide the walking stick and I'll kick your ass with it!" Gramps threatens. "It wouldn't be the first time and I'm sure it won't be the last!"

I smile, looking at Aston and tuning the conversation out a little as they continue to banter back and forth. His body and expression are relaxed, his smile easy, and his eyes light. This is the real Aston, the one he doesn't show. He's happy and playful, yet there's an underlying shadow to him.

If I ever had any doubt whether or not I was falling in love with Aston Banks, it's been completely wiped out.

There is no doubt. Here in the place he spent the happier years of his childhood sitting across from the man who made him into the incredible person he is today, there is only certainty.

Aston's expression darkens slightly, and I listen again.

"Gramps ..."

"I just want to know if you went."

"No. I didn't go and I don't plan to."

I look between the two, trying not to appear nosey – very hard when you feel like a third wheel.

"It might do you good."

"I'm not ready."

"It's been thirteen years, boy."

"I don't care if it's been thirteen or thirty, Gramps.

I'm not ready!" Aston stands and leaves the room, leaving his Gramps sighing.

The old man turns his face toward the window, his own shadows passing over his face. His eyes flick to me, hovering on my face for a moment. "Did he tell you? About himself?"

"Some," I reply honestly. "He got so far and … It was too much."

He nods his head, his gaze going back to the window. "I got him when he was six – the day they found out his mom had died. She was my baby. My only child. Losing her near killed me but he gave me something to live for. I had to protect him and give him the life she couldn't.

"He spent two days in hospital while he was checked out. He was underweight, dirty, and completely starving. But that wasn't the worst. There was a big gash on his palm with tiny pieces of glass in that had been left, scratches, and healing cuts across his legs, and a huge bruise on his back." He looks at me, and I don't try to disguise my horror.

"How could …" I trail off, putting my hand to my mouth as what he just said processes in my mind, and I shake my head.

I try to process it but I just can't imagine it. I can't imagine the pain Aston must have been in, both mental and physical. It makes me feel sick to my stomach, and I flatten my other hand over it like it'll stop the churning inside.

"He blames his mom for what happened. He blames

her for never protecting him – but I'm the one that should be blamed. I knew she wasn't fit to keep him, yet I left it anyway. His gran died when he was four and I was stuck in a loop of grief." He looks back at the window, and I follow suit, seeing Aston leaning against a tree. "I should be blamed for not protecting him."

"You didn't know what was happening, did you?"

"No."

The sadness coming off of him wraps around me and hurts me as much as Aston's does. I can see in the slump of his shoulders the guilt he's been carrying around for all these years, and in the downturn of his lips how much he really feels he's to blame. And it makes me mad. I hate that this innocent and loving old man feels that way because of the cruel and selfish actions of complete and utter bastards.

I sit up straighter. "Then how can you be blamed for something you knew nothing about? You took him in and brought him up to be the person he is today, and as much as he doesn't believe it, he's a credit to you. He doesn't see it, but he is. You did your best to make your daughter's wrongs right again. You could have walked away and left him to the state, but you didn't, and I for one think that makes you an incredible person."

His voice breaks. "You're very wise, Megan."

"It's the books." I turn my head, and we both share a small smile. "You mentioned about him going somewhere . . ."

"His mom's grave. I try every year to get him to go,

but he always says he's not ready. Stubborn little ass." He bangs his fist against the arm of his chair.

"I don't think he's accepted what happened to him. I don't think he's let himself deal with it."

"I hope he can. I hope *you* can deal with it." Gramps looks at me seriously, his gray eyes like granite. "It's not easy, what he's dealt with. What you know is only a small part of the crap my boy went through."

"I can deal with it," I reassure him. "And I can help him deal with it. I want to."

"I like you," he says suddenly. "You come across as a total romantic, but you have a kick-ass, hard edge to you. You won't take his shit, will ya?"

"I never have taken his shit, and I don't intend to start now." I smirk.

"Do me a favor?" Gramps leans forward. "One day, get him to his mom's grave. Even just for a minute. And for God sake, don't let the pretty ass walk all over you. He thinks he's Mr. Darcy."

"Then call me Elizabeth." I smile.

Chapter Sixteen - Aston

Why did he have to bring it up? Of all the things he could talk about, he brings her up. Every fucking time! I don't want to talk about her. Not to him. He doesn't understand. He doesn't know the same person I did. His ideals are different to mine.

His memories are a thousand miles apart from mine.

I kick at the sand, pulling my jacket tighter around my body, and Megan speaks for the first time since we left Gramps' house and drove north where no one would find us. "You okay?"

I shake my head. "No. Every time. Every fucking time he brings her up. I thought he wouldn't in front of you, but he did."

"He has his own pain," she says softly. "It doesn't excuse it, but he does. He feels guilty for what happened to you – that he couldn't stop it."

My mind reels, and I look down at her. "He told you that?"

She nods, letting her hand drop from my back, and stands in front of me. I stop.

"You've never let him tell you." She reaches up and cups my face. "He hurts too, Aston. You both hurt. It's not something that will go away, but you can't let it rule your lives. If you let pain rule you you'll get lost in it."

"What if I'm already lost?"

"You're not lost. You're hiding but you're not lost. I won't let you get lost."

I let my hands come up to rest on her back and pull her into me. "What if there's no map?"

"Then I'll get lost with you," she whispers. "I won't let you let them win, Aston. I won't let you get sucked in by those demons. I care too much to let that happen."

And she does. I can hear it in her voice.

She wraps her arms around my neck, and I hold her to me tighter, our foreheads resting against each other.

"I'll try, Megs," I promise. "I can't say I won't, but as long as you're here, I think I'll be okay."

"And you'll talk to your Gramps? Just once?"

"I'll think about it. How about we just focus on stopping me from getting lost for a bit?"

"You just need a place to aim for, that's all. You need a place to go to."

"Go on then." I smile. "Give me a place."

"Okay." She pauses for a second, closing her eyes and chewing her lip.

"I'm waiting . . ." I tease her.

Her blue eyes open, shocking me with their vitality. "Aim for the moon, because even if you miss, you'll land among the stars."

"I don't need to aim for the sky. The only star I'll ever need is standing right in front of me." I brush my lips over hers. "Maybe the place I need to aim for is nowhere other than where I am right now."

"Maybe I'd go with you wherever you ended up."

"Maybe I'd never ask that of you."

"Maybe you wouldn't need to ask. Maybe you'll never need to ask me for anything, because I'll always be here." She silences my upcoming argument by pressing her lips firmly against mine, holding me prisoner in her kiss. Her fingers tangle in my hair, her body fitting against mine perfectly.

My arms tighten around her waist, one of my hands moving up her back to cup the back of her head. She stands on her tiptoes and her tongue meets mine, never relenting in the pressure of her movements.

This girl is sliding between the cracks of me and gripping hold of the mismatched pieces before tearing them apart. She's studying them, getting to know them, to know me, and then she's carefully lining them all back up and holding them together.

What she'll never know is she's the glue that holds it together.

She's the glue that holds me together.

~

"So it's Sunday evening and we're on a deserted, dark beach in Northern California in the freezing cold, eating ice cream," Megan summarizes, running her finger around the top of her cone and licking it off.

"That sounds about right."

"And why are we eating ice cream instead of oh, having a coffee in Starbucks?" She raises an eyebrow at me.

I shrug. "I don't think they have a Starbucks in ... Wherever the fucking hell we are."

"Wherever we are? Oh, God. Remind me never to let you drive anywhere again."

"Let me?"

"Yes. Let you."

I scoop my arm around her waist and pull her into me. "You didn't let me do anything. I didn't see you offering to drive."

"Why would I offer to drive when you could do it for me?"

"But you just said ..." I shake my head, smiling at her playful grin. "Never mind. I don't think it's even worth trying to fucking understand."

"No, it's not." She beams, kissing me quickly and scooting away. "I'm just one of those people you'll never understand."

"That's because you're complicated."

"I am not complicated!"

"If you were simple, I'd be able to understand you."

She finishes the ice cream and throws the cone toward the trash as we come to edge of the beach. "You win."

"You didn't eat the cone?" I ask.

"I don't like the cones." She hops up onto the hood of the car, her legs hanging over the front.

"So why do you order ice cream cones?" I stand between her legs, and she hooks them round my waist, sliding into me.

"Because I like the ice cream," she says with a furrow in her brow. "Why else?"

I grin, and a fat raindrop falls on the car. Another follows it, and another, and another, and she squeals as one falls on her cheek.

Her hands push at my shoulders and she releases my waist as she tries to get away. I laugh as it rains harder, the cold drops soaking us in seconds. My tee shirt clings to my skin and my eyes flick to the drops of water sliding their way down Megan's chest, disappearing below the neck of her shirt. I take her hands from my waist and slide my fingers between hers, still laughing.

"Aston, no! Let me up! It's raining!"

"And?" I ask. "You're already soaking wet." She wriggles against me, her center rubbing against my jeans and causing the blood in my body to rush downwards. She wriggles once more and pauses, looking up at me when she realizes my dick is rock hard.

"Did I, er, do that?" She batters her eyelashes.

"Mhmm," I hum out, leaning into her.

"But the rai–"

My lips capture her mouth in a crushing kiss. My body is taut against hers as I lean forward, pushing her against the hood of the car. Our wet shirts rub together and hers rides up slightly. Our hands hit the car above her head and she gasps, my tongue meeting hers as I hold her hands still, my hips pinning hers. She moves her legs up, hooking them over my hips and clutching them around my waist. Her back arches into me so every inch of us really is touching.

Rain continues to beat down, covering us both as our tongues battle each other, sweeping and caressing. I release her hands, grip her wrists with one hand, and slide my free one down her wet body. Her shirt is slightly drier where it's against the car, and I run my hand along the part of her back not touching the hood. My fingers tickle and tease her, my thumb running just inside the back of her jeans, feeling the strap of her thong. My hips press into hers, and in this second, all good thoughts are gone.

A wet Megan – in more ways than one – is sending my dick into overdrive, and it's the only part of me thinking right now.

She gasps as I run my nose down her neck, breathing heavily against her slick skin.

"Megs–"

"Do you need me, or do you need what I can give you?" she asks bluntly, making my head snap back.

I get it.

"You," I reply honestly, looking into her eyes. "I fucking need *you.*"

"And if someone catches us?"

"Do you see anyone around?" I let her up, holding her against me and cupping her ass in my hands. "You're gonna have to open the car door, 'cause my hands are full."

I carry her round, my dick straining against my jeans, and she opens the door. I all but drop her in, and she sprawls on the back seat. I climb in after her, shutting the door, and lean over her. Her breathing is heavy as she gazes up at me through heavy eyelids.

I drop my head and kiss the spot beneath her ear, letting my mouth go down and down until it reaches the swell of her boobs. My tongue flicks out and runs inside her low-cut shirt and bra, reaching until it flicks against her nipple. She whimpers, clutching at my back, and I reach in and undo the buttons down the front of her body.

Her shirt falls away, revealing her body, and I keep kissing her, even as my hands fall to her jeans and begin to peel the wet material away down her thighs. I sit up, tugging it off the rest of the way, and she kicks the ceiling.

"Shit," she hisses, dropping her head back slightly. I laugh slightly, running my hands up her legs. She grabs fistfuls of my shirt and yanks me forward. "You shut up and kiss me."

"Fuck yes," I answer, taking her mouth with mine. Her fingers flick down my stomach, slipping under my shirt and caressing my stomach until they finally unclip the button on my jeans. She pushes my jeans down with her feet and pushes her body against mine.

My dick jumps at the contact, and I mutter a garbled curse into her mouth, ripping my boxers down and sliding her thong to the side. My fingers slip along and inside her tightness easily, and in seconds I replace my fingers with my cock and push into her. Her legs tighten around my waist and she grabs at my lower back, taking me in one easy swoop.

Judging by the constant clench of her muscles and

the wetness surrounding me, sex outside turns Megan on.

My fingers dip into her wet hair, my tongue dips into her mouth, and our hips grind together rhythmically.

In this deserted place where no-one knows her, where no-one knows me, we are as one.

And I realize it really is her I need.

~

Mommy was mad. I'd heard her shouting at him for a long time. I didn't know what many of the words meant, but they were words Mommy said were naughty and only for grown-ups. Words I mustn't say.

"They're coming tomorrow!" Mommy shouted. "What am I supposed to tell them this fucking time?"

"I don't fuckin' know! He's five years old – he fell out of a damn tree for all I care!"

"And got a black eye? From what? A freakin' tree root?!"

"Think of something!" he yelled at her, his feet stomping against the floor. Mommy always said not to stomp. Stomping is naughty. "They always believe you anyway!"

"Where are you going?"

"I'm leaving this fucking shithole before you get a black eye to match your little bastard of a son's!"

The door slammed. I jumped, rubbing Bunny's ear against my cheek. Soft.

I didn't like this man. I didn't like any of the men,

but he was the most horrible. He was really big and had lots of funny pictures all over his arms. I asked him what they were once and he shouted at me. I just wanted to see the pictures.

"Fuck! Fucking useless jackass!" Mommy yelled the naughty words and the door slammed after her.

I didn't mind her going. She was going to get money for food, she said. She said she had to work, but usually a nasty man stayed with me, drinking horrible beer.

I got up and pushed my door open slightly, looking around. I was really alone and it was dark. I didn't like the dark. The horrible men said big scary monsters were in the dark ready to eat little boys like me.

I looked toward the kitchen, shaking, my stomach hurting. I wanted to eat something. I was hungry. Mommy didn't have any food this morning, apart from a biscuit she gave me. Just a plain biscuit. I wanted some gravy.

I hugged Bunny even closer and looked around again. Maybe if I looked I could find some food.

Someone knocked at the door and I screamed. The big scary monsters. I started to cry and ran back into my room, pushing the door shut. I took my blanket from my bed and crawled under the bed, moving right to the back corner. My blanket wrapped around me and I curled into a ball.

No one ever found me here.

I was safe from the monsters.

Darkness. Monsters.

I pat the bed beside me. *The bed. Not the floor.*

I lean over, turning my bedside lamp on, and look around. My room – in the frat house. At college. In Berkeley – not my tiny room in San Francisco. No monsters, no men, no Mom. Just me, alone.

I bury my face in my shaking hands, adrenaline still running rife from my dream.

Fell from a tree. And they fucking believed it. The asshole had put his fist in my face for the first ever time, and all because I'd walked in front of the television and he'd missed a touchdown. That was all it took, five seconds, and I had another bruise, another memory, another scar to add to the collection.

And she still never did anything about it. She still covered it up. She still never checked on me.

Monsters.

It amazes me I was so fucking afraid of monsters that didn't exist. The real monsters were the tattooed, alcohol and drug dependent dicks she brought home again and again. They were the monsters – not the things a five year old boy's mind could conjure up.

The monsters in my mind then were much less worse than the ones I faced daily. They were nicer than the monsters I still face now.

I roll over, leaving the light on, and bring my knees to my chest. My thick blankets cover me the way my thin ones used to, and I curl up the way I used to under the bed. My need to protect myself, to protect my body

outweighs all else.
    In my mind, I am five again.

Chapter Seventeen - Megan

And we're back to it.

Another day of lies. Another day of pretending. Another day of wishful glances, discreet smiles, and banter with an underlying meaning only we understand.

Another day I have to remind myself that we *chose* this. We chose to be secret and not tell Braden. I'm just not sure how much longer we can keep it this way. Someone will find out eventually no matter how careful we are.

Hell, Kay and Lila are already halfway there.

"Just tell me who," Lila begs me. "I won't tell anyone, I swear."

"It's not a big deal. It was just one night. You guys are always telling me I need to get some, and I have, so leave it at that."

"You're kiddin' me!" Kay exclaims. "I want the details!"

"Maybe I don't want to give you the details."

"Maybe I can keep buggin' the shit out of you until you give them to me."

"Maybe I still won't give you the details." I shake my head. "Seriously, you guys, I'm not giving you what you want."

Maddie grins. "Stubborn."

"No, just private." I wink.

"Boring," Lila counters. "Boring is what it is." She sighs. "I and Maddie have shared our deets before, Kay has given us enough to write a damn book, and it's only you left to share – which you haven't this year. At all."

"There's nothing to share!" I protest, ignoring the guilt at lying yet again. I know full well there's a *lot* to share. "It just happened. It's not going to be mentioned again, so there we go. Conversation over." I check the time on my watch and grab my books, standing up. "I have to get to class. I'll see you later."

"What are you hiding, Megan Harper?" Lila yells after me.

I shake my head, chewing the inside of my lip, and keep walking. *Nothing,* I want to yell over my shoulder. *Aston,* is the word that crawls up my throat. I stay silent, making my way through the few people still milling through the hallways laughing and joking.

I turn the corner to the stairwell, and Aston is standing at the bottom of the stairs. I double-take as he looks around the empty area and walks toward me. His eyes find mine. His broken, weak eyes. My stomach knots, and I'm relieved when he wraps his arms around my neck and buries his face in the hair falling around my neck.

My arms slide around his waist, and I hold him with the tightness he holds me, trying to ignore the heavy, deep breaths he's taking. Trying to ignore the heaving of his chest and the shaking of his body. He nudges my hair aside and kisses my neck softly, breathing in deeply. I pull my face back and look into his eyes. He blinks once and dips his head. His whole body tenses when his lips crush mine and he's shaking with more than just his pain. He's shaking with the need to let it all out but not being able to. He releases me suddenly and walks the way I just came.

I stare after him, my heart feeling like a lead weight in my chest as reality sinks in. He said I make it better, take the pain away. I'd bet anything he spent the night tormented by his past, by the nightmares and flashbacks he tries to run from. Telling me on Saturday, then the conversation with his Gramps on Sunday must have been the trigger.

And five seconds is all I get to hold him. Five risky, stolen seconds and one desperate kiss is all I can have to take the pain away.

I shoulder my bag and head up the stairs to class, unable to take him off my mind. All I can see in front of me are his eyes. Even as I sit at my desk and open my books, the words blur and I picture the pain etched onto his face. I picture the scars I'll never understand.

Because he was right. The worst scars are the ones you carry inside, the ones you hide from the rest of the world.

But I don't have the scars. I lived a happy, sheltered life in a nice area, a million miles away from the reality of some people's lives. The most horrible part of my childhood was my mom filtering my reading material and the best when Nanna told her to give it up and let me read what I wanted. I'm naïve and blind to the lives of people outside my own. I know this now, and I'll never understand Aston's pain. I'll never understand the things that circle his mind each day, the words that poison it.

"'Hell is empty and all the devils are here'," my professor quotes from her copy of *The Tempest*, the words slashing through my musings. "A powerful statement – and very potent in a time where belief of the devil was very real. What did Shakespeare mean by his words?"

"He meant exactly what he said," I say, my eyes focusing on the fifty-something woman pacing the front of the room. "'The devils are here.' Whether or not he believed in God he would have believed that each of us have free will as the bible teaches us – the free will to be either good or evil. The people that chose to be evil, to steal, beat, murder, they were the devils. They still are."

"So you agree, Megan?"

"How can you not? I'm by no means religious, nor do I pretend to be, but I'm not blind to the world. If there is a God, a greater good, then there must be a devil and a greater evil to balance it out. The greater evil is in the people sitting on both death row and a park bench. If there is a hell, it's most definitely empty. Ask anyone who has been unfortunate enough to come into contact with one of those people and has demons of their own left over. They'll tell you that the devils are here disguised as one of us."

"So you're saying you could be sitting among devils and not know it?" Her eyebrow raises and she pauses in her pacing.

"You walk among them daily, whether or not you

realize it. We all do, and we probably know someone that has demons inside their mind and not know it."

My professor nods, moving onto someone else.

Demons. Just like Aston has.

Demons from the evil that spawned them.

Shakespeare was right. If there is a devil, he's definitely on this Earth.

~

Green-gray eyes. Chestnut brown hair with a hint of copper. Nice broad shoulders and the lingering of a summer tan on his skin. And as boring as a lecture on psychics in a monotone voice.

Which, in fact, could be what he's talking to me about right now.

I'm going to kill Lila for this one.

"I'm sorry." I come back to the here and now. "What did you say?"

He bristles a little. "Did you listen to any of that?"

"Um." A slight flush rises on my cheeks. "Not really. I'm sorry. I'm not great company right now. I have a few things, er, going on."

"Do you want to talk about it? It helps, you know."

Dude, I can't even remember your name. I'm not about to tell you my life story.

"No, no, it's fine. Thanks." I attempt a smile through gritted teeth, hoping I'm a better actress than I think I am. "Maybe we should just finish up here."

"Sure." He waves toward the counter for our small bill, and I swallow my relieved sigh. He pays it despite my protests, and we step outside. "So, Megan …"

Oh, no. Please don't.

"Mm?" I hope I don't look as worried as I feel. Crap. I'm a terrible person.

"I know you're not in the right kind of mood tonight, but maybe we could go out again sometime?"

Shit. "Um." I scratch behind my ear. What's his name? *Double shit.* "Look, I'm not sure what Lila told you, but she's kind of setting me up. It's not you, I'm sure you're a lovely guy, but I'm just not looking for anything right now."

He smiles widely and shrugs a shoulder. "Yeah, she mentioned it. It was worth a shot though, right?"

"Uh, sure." I smile again. "I think I need to go and have a chat with her, actually. Thanks for the meal."

"You're welcome." He waves as he walks away, and I begin the walk back to campus, thinking over what I have to say to Lila.

I know how it will go. She'll demand to know why I can't possibly have any more dates, and I'll make up some floozy excuse that's about as believable as me saying I'm a Vegas stripper. But I can't do this anymore. I can't pretend to enjoy these dates. It's not fair on me, Aston, or on the guys I have to go out with.

I jog the final stretch to campus as rain lightly begins to fall. A shiver runs down my spine as yesterday comes back to me. Nothing can compare to the way I felt as Aston pinned me against the hood of his car, kissing me like I'm his one requirement to live.

Maybe that's why I can't consider anyone else, why every date Lila sends me on will be futile.

Maybe it's because when I look at other guys all I see is him.

I shake my hair out as I walk into the dorm room. Lila looks up from her books and grins. "How did it go? I gotta say, I expected you to be back a lot later–"

"This has to stop," I say bluntly. "This dating thing. I won't do it anymore."

"Why? Was he an ass?"

I shrug my jacket off. "No, he was nice. Just like the last one. Shit, they're all nice, Li. I just don't care about any of them."

"Let me guess – they're not your Mr. Darcy?" She raises an eyebrow, and I throw myself onto the bed.

"Precisely."

"Let me help you find him."

"I don't need your help to find him."

"Megs, I just want you to find someone who makes you happy."

"I'm happy!"

"I didn't say you weren't but I want you to find your Darcy. I want to help you do that."

"I don't need your help!"

"Megs–"

"I've already found him!"

Fuckshitohmygod. I slap my hands over my mouth,

my eyes widening to the size of dinner plates. Why did I say that? Fuck. Fuck. Now I've done it. This is it. Cover blown.

Well done, Megan Harper. You absolute fucking idiot.

Lila's eyes widen slowly and she drops her pen onto the bed. Her jaw drops open, and I feel like everything is moving in slow motion. *Why the hell did I have to say that?!*

"What?" she asks. "You found him? Who is he?"

"Um. Did I say that?" I laugh nervously. "Really? Ha. Um. I didn't. I don't. Shit." I fall sideways on the bed and bury my head in my pillow, my heart pumping furiously.

"Nuh-uh!" she exclaims. "You are not saying that and then just flaking on me, Megan Harper!" Her bed springs squeak and she gets up. Her hands wrap around my arm and she yanks me up. I pull the pillow up with me, keeping my face covered, but she tugs it away. I smack my hands over my face.

"Um, I lied?" I try lamely. "To get you to stop?"

"No way! No. Way. I can't believe you found your Darcy and you didn't tell me."

Yeah … "I kinda … Can't. Tell you." I drop my hands.

"I'm your best friend! What do you mean, you can't tell me?"

"Exactly what it says on the tin. I can't tell you."

"What are you? Romeo and Juliet having a secret romance? Forever destined to be star-crossed?" She snorts, jumping back on her bed. I bite my lip, and she looks at me seriously. "Megan."

"Um." Is that really all I have? Freaking "*um*?"

"Oh my god. You're not …?"

"Um." Again with it! I study English every day and I can't think of a better word than that? This is going from bad to worse.

"No. Oh God," Lila mutters. "Oh God."

"I have a right to remain silent, right?" I pull my knees up and release my lip, replacing it with my thumbnail. I chew on it for a moment as she stares at me in shock. "Like in a police interrogation? I don't have to answer without a lawyer."

"You are! You're babbling. You're such a bad liar." She takes a deep breath and shakes her head. "I don't know whether to hug you or slap you."

"I plead the fifth."

"Megs, are you and–"

"Please don't ask me anything, Lila," I whisper, looking at her earnestly. "I don't want to lie to you anymore."

Silence stretches. I swallow. Chew my nail. Tap my foot. Lila stands and paces. I chew my nail. She paces.

"Aston," she mutters, sitting back down. "When? How?"

I shake my head.

Recognition dawns on her. "When Braden took Maddie home. And since … He hasn't slept with anyone. He's always with you, isn't he? The weekends – when I'm at the frat house – he's here. That's why no one has seen him. Damn." She shakes her head. "You've really pulled this off without anyone finding out?"

She's not going to drop this. I know it, but this is all my fault. Time to face the music.

"Somehow. But, Lila, you can't tell anyone," I beg. "I mean it. No one can know. You are the only person that knows."

"And it's the real thing? Not just sex?" She tilts her head to the side.

I nod and trace my finger along the pattern on my quilt. "There's more to him than meets the eye. We're not just sex. I . . ."

"He's your Darcy," she says simply. "He's the rain to your drought. The every to your thing. Your soul mate decided by the universe, right?"

"And that's why you can't tell anyone," I insist. "No one. Not even Ryan."

"And Braden really doesn't know?"

I snort. "Do you think we'd be secret if Braden knew? Braden would flatten the house with his anger."

"Why? You're both his best friends. Y'know what? I don't damn well understand him."

"Because I'm like his sister and Aston is a playboy incapable of feeling anything than what's inside his pants. At least that's the case in his mind."

Lila sits back on the bed, letting out a long breath. "But you know Braden *will* find out, right? Sooner or later, Megs. He will know."

"I know. I just hope it's later."

"Why not? Why not get it over and done with?"

Because I'm a chicken. I'm a wimp. Because I know I've fucked up majorly and I can't bring myself to admit it. And finally . . .

"Because I'm gonna need a freakin' good excuse as to why we've kept it quiet for so long."

Chapter Eighteen - Aston

Gramps' house has never looked more daunting. The house I really grew up in and the only home I've ever known is now one of the scariest places I'll ever have to face.

Inside this happy place is a box full of demons ready to be unleashed on the world, and that's something I can't think about. I can't think over whether or not it's a good idea for me to be here. I can't decide if this is the right decision for me right here, right now.

I just know this conversation has to happen. I can't stay locked in my past but I'll never be able to move on if Gramps can't. I won't be able to get past it if it's my own damn ignorance keeping him locked in place.

"What you doin' here in the middle of the week?" Gramps grumbles as I push the door open and walk into the house.

"Come to talk to you," I reply, dropping onto the sofa next to him.

He drags on his cigar, the smoke swirling, and pierces me with his eyes. "You've been sittin' out there in that pretty boy car for long enough. Whatchu wanna talk about?"

I take a deep breath and look away, knowing that the next word will change everything. "Mom."

He doesn't say anything. He exhales, blowing out

smoke, and I see him shift slightly. "Thought you didn't care about her."

"Maybe I want to know, now. Maybe I'm ready to listen to what you have to say." I turn my face back to him slowly. "Maybe it's time we were both honest about the shit inside our heads, Gramps."

"Megan's a good one, for sure. She made you come here didn't she?"

I shake my head. "She made me realize I can't live in the past forever but she didn't make me do anything. I came here on my own."

"She knows you're here?"

"No."

Gramps shifts again and sits back, leaving his cigar to rest on the ashtray. His elbows rest on the arms of the chair and he links his fingers in front of him. "What do you want to know?"

I tuck my hands under my legs the way I used to when I was a little boy and he was about to start a lesson or read me a story. In many ways the conversation we're about to have is both. The naked truth of the story and a lesson in that truth.

"Whatever you have to tell me. Whatever you think I should know."

"The first thing you need to know is that your mom wasn't always the person you knew. Until she was sixteen she was the perfect daughter. A first grade student, polite, friendly … I couldn't have asked for a better baby girl. She was the kinda girl that would bake you sugar-free cookies if you told her you couldn't have sugar. Then she hit junior year and got mixed with the wrong people.

"Now that ain't no excuse for what she did, but they were a big influence on her. I know I can't blame them – she made the choices she did. They weren't forced upon her. There's no excusing the life she created for herself – or for you.

"The day she came home and said she was pregnant was a crazy day. Me and your Gran, we had a mix of emotions. We were gonna have us a lil' grandbaby, but it was at the cost of *our* baby. She was only just seventeen, and we'd never imagined a weekend at her friend's would have ended up that way. Still, we tried to help her any way we could."

"When did you know …? About the drugs?"

"About five months in. Your Gran went with her to the scan, and you were this tiny little thing on screen. You were small the whole pregnancy. Your mom's doctor knew from blood tests she'd done them but she swore she stopped. Eventually, the doc managed to get out of her she was still doing them, and so started the program to wean her off while you were still inside her, to minimize the damage she could be causing you."

"But they couldn't see that on the scans?"

Gramps shakes his head. "No, boy. Physically you were fine. Small but fine. Mentally? They wouldn't know exactly how the drugs would affect you until you were older, speaking and moving and all that."

"So you tried to stop her?"

"Course we did. She was still under eighteen so we limited the time she spent out without either of us. Somehow she still managed to get the darn drugs. She slipped them by us. The day you were born five weeks early, this tiny little four pound baby that was as long as my damn arm, was the second best day of my life. Don't you doubt that. I remember lookin' at your Gran and sayin' to her, 'May, this boy here is *my* boy. When he's big, we'll go on them fishing trips I love, and I'll teach him about a real football team, then I'll teach him how to treat his lady right.'" Gramps pauses for a second, swiping at his eyes, and I swallow. "I promised there and then I'd never let anythin' happen to you, but I did."

"It wasn't your fault, Gramps."

"I should have taken you there and then!" He bangs his fist against the arm of his chair. "I never shoulda let her have full custody of you, but I thought she was better. I thought my baby girl was coming back." Tears stream down his cheeks, and I slip off the sofa and kneel in front of him. "I thought you'd be fine. Even when she took you away and moved out when you were almost two, I thought you'd be fine. You always seemed fine. We saw you every other weekend until you were four. Then your Gram died of her stroke and I was alone. I forgot everything except the fact I'd lost my wife, my best friend, my soul mate. I forgot you."

"You never forgot me, Gramps. You were always there, even when you weren't."

"Anyway. Two years later the police turn up, tell me

they've identified a dead body as my daughter, and there's a six year old boy that needs a home or he'll get put into care. No way was I letting my boy get abused by the system. I'd failed my baby girl. I wasn't about to fail you any more than I already had."

"You didn't fail me." I touch his arm and he looks up at me, his gray eyes watery. I bite back my own tears. "You didn't, Gramps. You saved me – you taught me how to live. You took me on those fishing trips, taught me about football, and taught me how to treat my girl right. You took the shit my life was and turned it into something entirely different. You didn't fail me, not for a second."

"I should have–"

"You never raised a fist to me. You never whipped my back with a belt. You never kicked my stomach until I vomited. You never smacked my head against the corner of a kitchen table." My whole body shakes as the images flash in quick succession through my mind. Different men, different days, different times. Different ways of beating me, all leaving the same scars. "You. Didn't. Do. That. You didn't even know. But she did. She knew. She lied to the hospital, CPS, everyone – it was always blamed on me. You didn't know. You couldn't stop what you didn't know about."

"Doesn't stop the guilt, son."

"Then remember what you *did* do." My gray eyes meet his properly. "Remember what you did teach me. I'm the person I am because of you." I pause, knowing the next words about to fall off my tongue are the total truth, and I'm saying them to myself as much as I am him. "You showed me Darcy and Elizabeth, you introduced me to his arrogance. Until recently, I was Darcy. I didn't give a shit about anyone other than myself. Then there was Megan. Without you showing me Darcy, I never would have thought she could have been anything more than one night. You showed me how Darcy loved Elizabeth and because of that you taught me how to love. You taught me how to love Megan the way Darcy loved Elizabeth. You did that. No one else. Just you."

Gramps reaches forward and hugs me, his body shaking as he cries into my shoulder. This is what I've denied him because I was so caught up in my own fucking pain. My best friend – everything he kept inside to keep me happy. I hug him tighter, letting my own tear fall from my eye.

"Know something, boy?" he mumbles, sitting back and composing himself.

"What, Gramps?"

"Your Gran would be damn proud of the man you've become."

And I believe him.

For the first time, I truly believe she would be.

~

Megan is sitting with her back against a tree trunk, her hair swept to one side and showing the smooth, tanned skin on one side of her neck. Her legs are bent making her jeans look tighter than they are normally, and as she wraps her arms around her waist, I want to be the one doing it. I want my arms around her waist, her back against my chest, and her head resting on my shoulder while I lean the side of my face against her bare neck.

Instead I'm lying on my side trying not to look at her. Trying to ignore her. Trying to pretend I need anything other than to hold her in my arms until the next ice age and we freeze there together.

"You're telling me the Chargers are on better form than the Cowboys?" Braden shakes his head. "Fuck off are they! Romo is playing his ass off this season."

Lila opens her mouth. "It's a–"

Ryan slaps his hand over it. "Don't. Say. It."

"Game," Megan finishes for her. "A game, boys. It is *a game*. I know you're in love with your boys, and Bray, if you were gay you'd be after Romo's supposedly shit hot ass, but it is just a game. And he's playing shit, for what it's worth."

"What is it?" I smirk at her. "I don't think I quite got that."

"Do I need to spell it for you? What, did you not get master hearing with your smart-ass GPA?" She raises her eyebrows. "'Cause that's gotta cause you some problems."

"I'm pretty sure my hearing is going because of the amount of times I've had a girl screaming in my ear."

Braden snorts, and Maddie slaps his thigh. "Don't encourage him!"

"I was just . . . Never mind." He hides his smirk.

"You know screaming is relative, right?" She runs the pad of her thumb across her bottom lip. "It doesn't necessarily mean they were having a good time. I mean, don't girls usually scream in horror movies?"

Lila's shoulders shake as she laughs silently, and Maddie bites her lip. I watch Megan steadily, taking in the spark in her blue eyes and the gentle curve of her lips that only grows as I keep watching her. My own lips twitch, and I jump up.

"Watch your smart mouth, Megan," I warn her. "My last offer is still open."

Chapter Nineteen - Megan

My mouth drops open, not from what he said, but because he threw it out so carelessly in front of the others – especially Braden.

Aston grins and winks at me. He turns, stretching his arms over his head as he walks in the direction of the house. I watch him go, struck into silence, and ignore Lila's gaze burning into the side of my head.

"His last offer?" Braden says tightly, his eyes resting on me.

"He offered to teach me the difference between a slapped ass and a spanked one," I mutter. "He's a prick."

"Caveman. Rein it in," Maddie orders, tapping his cheek and standing up.

"In," he mutters in response.

"Good. Keep it that way." She kisses his cheek, and Ryan and Lila stand.

"I'll see you after class, Megs." Lila looks at me pointedly, and I nod. Yep. I'm so in for tonight.

We sit in silence as the others disappear, and I stare into the distance. It's the first time I've been alone with Braden since me and Aston got together, and for the first time in my life it feels like there's a gaping hole between us.

I know I put it there.

I also know I have to tell him. I could do it now.

Without Aston here. Where there are other people around.

I open my mouth to speak, explain it, but he beats me to it.

"Where have you been lately?"

"Huh?" I look at him. "I've been here, at college."

"Oh, ha ha. Very fucking funny," he says dryly, throwing a blade of grass at me. "No, I mean, like, SF. I thought you would have come with us."

I shrug a shoulder. "I just didn't feel like it. I had some work to catch up on too. Papers and stuff."

He nods. "Kyle said you dropped by Sunday morning to get one of your books."

"Yep. You had my Shakespeare book. Again."

"I will always have your Shakespeare book. I don't know how to complete a paper without your scribbled on books." He grins at me, flicking his hair away from his eyes.

"You need a hair cut," I point out. "And I know. Ever since eighth grade you've copied my crap. I have no idea why I let you do it."

"It's because I'm fucking brilliant, and you love me."

"And you still have the worst potty mouth of everyone I know."

He grins again. "It's why you love me, Megs. I'm the big brother you never had."

"I think you're the *reason* I never had a big brother," I reply dryly, smirking. "Mom saw you dragging me into the mud to make mud pies and climbing trees, and decided an adopted son was more than enough."

"I dragged you?" He laughs. "You dragged me more

times than I did you!"

Okay. So he might have a point there. "Let's face it, we were always gonna be trouble."

He clears his throat. "I'm not trouble."

"The cat, Braden. The cat."

"That wasn't trouble. That was me attempting to be a gentleman."

I smile, amused. "I'm not sure your mom thinks of it that way, even now."

"No, I explained it to her," he insists. "I told her it made me a gentleman for trying to give my favorite girl in the world what she wanted." I kick his foot playfully.

"Does Maddie know this?" I tease.

"Meggy." He looks at me seriously. "I love Maddie, but you're my best friend. You always have been and the only person that means more to me than Maddie is you. I love you in different ways, and Maddie knows she'll never be you, but she gets that. Besides, you can be my favorite in a different way."

I laugh and kick him again, shaking my head. "Is sex really all you ever think about?"

He pauses for a second, chewing his lip. "No. I just thought about food."

"Food and sex?"

"Xbox."

"Beer?"

"And that is why you're my best friend." He winks. "You get me."

"Someone has to understand you, Bray."

"Is Lila still sending you on those dates?"

I shake my head. "I told her after the last one, no more."

"Were they jackasses?"

"No, I just wasn't interested in any of them. I'm capable of picking my own love interests, you know."

"Shouldn't have any damn interests," he grumbles.

I clear my throat. "Remember our conversation about this? Do we need to go to caveman-speak? Megan, big girl. Take care of self. Braden watch and shut up."

Braden chuckles. "Does that mean no black eyes for anyone who sleeps with you?"

You owe your best friend a few. "No. No black eyes, no warnings, no demands of leaving me alone, and most definitely no caveman antics."

"I think all of those qualify as caveman antics as far as Maddie is concerned."

"I know. I was just spelling it out for you." I shrug.

"Gee, thanks a fuckin' lot." He shakes his head, standing up. I put my hand in his outstretched one, and he pulls me up. He starts to walk backwards toward the house. "I have to get to class. Get some last minute caveman antics in before anyone finds out."

"Braden Carter!" I call after his retreating body. "Don't you freakin' dare!"

He stops at the door, grins, and disappears inside. I shake my head, detouring around the house and taking the route away from the campus toward the bay.

Yet again I failed to tell him about me and Aston. A

few words is all it would take, but the longer we hide it the harder it is to find the words. The harder it is be honest.

Lying. I hate it – I hate lying to everyone about everything, because I don't want to hide us. I don't want to hide the way I feel about Aston. I don't want to hide him. I just don't want to hurt anyone and I know it will hurt Braden.

But the longer I keep it secret the more it will hurt him.

The breeze from the water drifts over me, chilling me, and I tug my sweater around my body tighter. My hair flies into my face and I push it away in vain.

Games. They're all good until someone gets hurt. Braden and Maddie's games were all good until they got hurt and both acted irrationally – him by walking away and her by running. Mine and Aston's games are all good until it gets out, which it will.

The truth always comes out.

I could walk away now. I could speak to Aston and tell him it's done, I can't do it anymore, but I'd still be lying then. I'd be lying because I can, because it's not done.

Lies. They're easy to keep track of until they begin spiraling and you begin spinning a web of them, too easy to get caught up in. Lies are all good until you look at who you're lying to.

The question is, is it better or worse to lie to yourself over your best friend?

~

"That was awkward today," Lila comments as she enters the room.

I look up from my book. "Welcome to my world."

"A world you created."

"Your tact amazes me," I say dryly. "Really, Li, just remind me. It doesn't play on my mind or anything. Nope, I'm totally oblivious to it."

"I don't get why you don't just admit it."

"No one asked?" I try, shrugging. I sigh. I don't know either. "I wish I knew, I really do. It's not as simple as it looks from the outside. You see it as a simple secret, something hidden for a simple reason. Simple. And it's not. It's not just boy meets girl and they fall in love. Its boy meets girl and all hell breaks loose, in his head and in reality."

"So you're telling me that Aston's head is stopping you being honest?" She raises an eyebrow in disbelief. I shut my book and put it on my bed next to me.

"You don't know him. You think you do – you all think you do, but you don't. To you he's just a girl-using, thinks-with-his-dick asshole to be avoided by anyone with any sense. I know different. I know he's not what he seems, and I know that what he seems is nothing more than an act to hide who he really is."

"Okay." She settles on the bed. "I don't know either way, so let's go with what you said. When does your pretending become reality? When does your act end,

Megs?"

I sigh and lean back against the wall. "I have no idea. I tried to tell Braden earlier – no, I did. Maybe not hard enough, but I tried. The words just wouldn't come. I keep thinking about how he'll look when he finds out I've lied to him."

"Doesn't matter when he finds out. He isn't gonna look any happier if he finds out today or next year."

"I just don't know how much longer I can hide it. It makes everything so hard. I need to help Aston, Lila, but having everything secret means I can't always be there and that hurts," I finish quietly. "I can see when he needs me and it hurts so damn bad."

She shrugs. "I know now. I can help. Keep everyone away from here or make excuses for you, back you up."

"I swear you were just telling me I needed to tell Braden."

"And you do." She sighs. "But it's clear you won't – or *can't*," she corrects at my annoyed look, "so I might as well help you. God help me because I *will* be killed when this all comes out, but at least I can feel like I'm keeping this secret for a reason."

"You don't have to do anything. I got myself into this mess. I just need to figure out how to help Aston, and then maybe everything else will just … Fall into place." I run my fingers through my hair, sighing deeply. "Maybe. Hopefully."

"Until everything falls into place, I'll help you. I'll make it so you can talk to Aston. I don't see it myself, I'm not gonna lie. But you care about him, and I care about you, so whatever."

I look at her for a second, taking in her honest expression, and smile slightly. "You're the best friend."

"Or the stupidest, when Braden finds out," she mutters and heads toward the bedroom.

"Li?" I ask. "You're not gonna tell him, are you?"

She stops at the bathroom door and looks at me over her shoulder. "I may not agree with you keeping it quiet, and I may not like the fact I know, but that doesn't mean I'm gonna tell him, Megs. I don't like your decision, but I respect it."

"Thank you."

"Besides," she continues. "If I tell him he'll kick *my* ass, and I'm the innocent one."

"There I was thinking you were doing it out the goodness of your heart!"

"No way." She grins. "I'm protecting my ass – and you make sure Aston knows about this so I can call in a favor in the future." She winks. I laugh, reaching for my phone.

Lila knows, I send to Aston.

What the fuck? How?

She guessed. It's not a total lie ...

And?

And nothing. She's not gonna say anything. She'll cover for us.

I don't like this, Megs.

Neither do I, but it's either she covers or we tell

Braden.

Let's stick with Lila for now.

We need to talk.

About?

You.

~

I sink into Aston's arms, sliding my hands under his shirt and flattening them against his back. His lips come down on mine firmly, and he sucks my bottom lip between his.

"What's Lila doing?" he murmurs.

"Lila took the others to crazy golf." I shrug, looking up at him. "Don't ask me. She kicked up a fuss to Ryan."

"Lila hates crazy golf. In fact, she hates any kind of sport."

"I know." I shrug again. "She said you owe her."

"Figures." He sighs and runs his fingers through my hair to the ends, kissing the end of my nose. "So tell me. What do we really need to talk about? 'You' isn't exactly informative."

I tug him toward the bed, and he sits down against the wall. My knees sit either side of him as I straddle him and lock my hands behind his neck. His hands rest on my bed, his fingers drawing tiny circles against my skin.

"You. Everything. There's more, Aston. I know there is."

His stomach tenses. "What do you want to know?"

"Everything," I whisper. "Everything that's left. However long it takes, however much it hurts … I'm here."

His chest heaves as he takes a deep breath, and his eyes fill with apprehension. Fear sparks in them. I've never thought of him as being scared of his past, of what he hasn't let himself think about, but he is. He's petrified.

"There isn't much left to tell, not about when I was a kid. It was the same thing over and over. Mom would sell herself for money, spend a minimal amount of it on food and bills if she could be bothered, and the rest on drugs and alcohol. She'd meet a guy, he'd watch me while she 'worked', and I'd usually get a bruise to add to my collection for something or another. Social Services would visit, the guy would leave, and she'd meet someone else, every other night going out and fucking some poor rich guy so she could keep putting the same old shit into her veins. That was it for six years. I'm glad I can only remember two years of it, even if they were the worst years."

His fingertips dig into my skin slightly, and I twist his hair around my fingers gently, looking at him intently.

"She couldn't parent. She didn't know how to. I was always an afterthought – and everything was blamed on me. She blamed it on me, the guys blamed it on me, and when you get taught everything is your fault, you start to believe it. Every cut or bruise was explained as me being a rough little boy to the social, and every cut or bruise was explained as me being a little no-good bastard to *me.* That was their reasoning. That I was good for nothing, no better than my mom." He pauses for a second, breathing harshly.

I move my hands to cup his face and rest my forehead against his, letting him calm down even as my own stomach twists. He closes his eyes in pain, and I can't begin to imagine the things that are playing out behind his eyes. All I can do is sit here with him, holding him to me, and ride it out.

"That's what I remember most, the things they said to me," he whispers. "It's like they enjoyed hurting me with words as much as they did with their fists. It was all the time. All the fucking time, Megs. I remember them always telling me I'd be no better than her, that sex was all she was good for so it would be all I was good for. Sex and drugs and alcohol – they said that was my life, and it would have been true. She never sent me to school because of the bruises, so eventually I would have ended up the same way if she hadn't died."

"How did she die?"

"Drugs. What else?" He shrugs a shoulder, moving his arms so they wrap around my body. "The official report states it was from an overdose of a bad batch of heroine. The drug had been tampered with, making it even more dangerous, and she accidentally overdosed. They reckon she'd been going through withdrawals and in her confused and desperate state she used more than she normally would have. She was found three blocks away from our apartment at a seedy bar, and I was found at home a day later. That's what Gramps said anyway. I remember it all as just one blur of time. Day and night were the same to me then. Mom slept during the day and left at night. I was left alone most of the time – except for a single weekly outing to the park to keep up appearances. That was the one day she cared about me."

His voice is so broken, so small, so lost. It's like he's regressed back into the mind of the six-year old he was and is seeing the world through his eyes again. I look at him, look into his sad eyes, and my heart clenches as a tear spills from his eye. I've seen him angry. I've seen him fight the demons. But I've never seen him cry, and this breaks my heart.

Seeing him cry is worse than I ever could have imagined.

Chapter Twenty - Aston

One tear falls, and another, and another.

The pain is real. It's old but real, always there, and it's finally breaking through. It's been held back for so long, but it's finally out. I'm starting to let go of the things that have killed me for years.

Megan's touch is warm and soft, comforting and safe, and as she pulls me into her, I let her. She doesn't speak. She doesn't do anything but just hold me. She reminds me I'm not alone, that I'm safe. As much as I need to hold her, I need her to hold me just as much. She grounds me and keeps me here. By focusing on her I'm reminded that I'm not six years old and afraid anymore. She stops the flashbacks consuming me. She makes that pain bearable.

"That's why I major in psych," I breathe out after a while of her holding me. "Because it means I can help kids like me that have all this shit in their heads. If I'd had someone to talk to when I was younger, I probably wouldn't be this fucked up now."

"You're not fucked up." She sits back and runs her thumbs across my cheeks, drying the tears there. "You had a hard life, Aston, but now you're dealing with it. You're proving, yourself, that all those men, they were wrong. By graduating school and coming here, you're proving them wrong. You did that. No one else."

"No. I'm always gonna be a little fucked up, Megs.

I'm still gonna wake in the night and wonder if I'm hiding under my bed or if I'm safe. I'm still gonna doubt myself every day, and I'm still gonna be a little broken, no matter what I do."

"But you'll also heal a little more every day," she says softly. "We'll find a way to help you deal with those nightmares and flashbacks, I promise. I'll help you, Aston."

Her blue eyes gaze into mine and her hair falls around our faces, hiding us from the rest of the world. I could lose myself in her eyes a thousand times over and still go back again. I could fall into her touch and never feel the need to get up, and I realize that's why she's so different to everyone else. She gives me what no one else ever has. She slowly pulled me from not caring about anything to caring about her. And she's made me realize so many things.

No matter what Mom's boyfriends said, I've proved them wrong. It was my own actions that got me to Berkeley – to meet Megan. When I went to live with Gramps he taught me everything, but it was me that pushed on through it, graduated high school and came to college.

It was me that made it so I could meet Megan.

I will never be like my mom because she never loved anyone except herself. I can never be that person, destined for a broken life of sex, drugs, and alcohol.

Because I'm completely in love with the girl right in front of me.

~

Here we are, back at the usual Friday nights I craved so much. Friday nights meant forgetting and giving in to physical feelings only. Friday and Saturday nights were the best nights, but now I just want to grab Megan and run. I want to take her away from this shit ass party.

Especially when Lila's fucked up plan to get her a date has made its way round the classes we all have and you have every Tom, Dick, and fucking Harry trying to get in there.

Every time one of those jackasses goes up to her, for a split second, I resent Braden and the fact he's the reason this relationship is fucking secret. I'd love to go over to her right now, grab her away from the dick in front of her and kiss her senseless in front of everyone to make my point. I'd do anything to take her away from them and show everyone where she belongs. Who she belongs to.

Because she is mine, and not in a possessive way. It's my arms she falls into, my lips she kisses, my heart she holds. All of that makes her mine.

Not the arrogant bastard's she's talking to.

I slam my bottle down, ignoring startled looks from around me, and push through the throngs of people. I deliberately nudge her back as I pass her and head to the stairs. My feet take them two at a time, flying up. I'm not watching that shit anymore. My room is silent, quiet, and I wait for her to come up.

I have no idea how long I have to wait. Too long and

I'll end up going back down there, too little and people will guess she's come after me. People will wonder why … But I don't know if I care anymore. I don't know if I can care anymore.

My door opens and closes.

"There has to be a good reason you just stormed up here like a girl on her period with no access to chocolate," Megan quips.

"I can't do this secret shit anymore, baby." I turn around and pin her with my eyes, briefly noticing how well her jeans hug her hips. "I can't be down there with you surrounded by assholes and not slip my arm around your waist and warn them off with my eyes. I can't fuckin' do it. Not now."

"It's never bothered you before."

"It's always bothered me! You think I've never cared when I've watched you laughing and joking with whoever it is trying to get inside your damn pants on that night?"

She steps forward. "I never said you didn't care! I said it never bothered you – and if it did you never showed me!"

"So if I walked up to a girl and started talking to her for the sake of keeping up appearances, you wouldn't be bothered by it, huh?" I look at her helplessly. "I can't watch them fucking ogle you, Megs. This secret relationship has gone on for too long. We have to come clean."

Her eyes widen a little. "We can't … Braden–"

"Will have to fucking deal with it!" I step in front of her, cupping the side of her face, and she rests her hands against my chest. "He'll have to deal with it. He'll have to accept it, because I'm not pretending anymore and I'm not giving you up for shit."

"He'll hate us," she whispers.

"The damage has already been done, baby. It's him or us."

She shakes her head, running her bottom lip between her teeth worriedly. "Braden." I hate the way she winces when she says his name.

"Then we have to tell him," I say softly, lowering my mouth to hers. "Now. We'll tell him now."

The door bursts open "Tell me what?"

Chapter Twenty-One - Megan

I jump away from Aston, my hand flying to my mouth when I see Braden standing there. His eyes flick between us, the blue in them slowly getting icier, his expression getting harder.

The tension in the room rockets. I can almost feel Aston tensing next to me, see the anger and realization flooding through Braden's body. I'm standing frozen, unable to do anything but wait. Unable to do anything but look at the anger and betrayal firing up in my best friend's eyes.

There are a thousand excuses rolling around my mind, but the cat really does have my tongue.

There's nothing than can excuse this.

And it's time to be honest.

"Ryan thought he saw you follow Aston up." Braden focuses his eyes on me. "I thought he was crazy. I told him it was some other poor fucker, but when a couple of the other guys agreed I said I'd come up just for a laugh. Because I didn't actually fucking think I'd find you up here in his goddamn bedroom!"

"Bray . . ." I whisper.

"How long?" He looks at Aston, his jaw tight. "How long have you been fucking her?"

"Braden!"

"It's not like that," Aston replies equally tight.

"Really? You expect me to believe that bullshit?" Braden yells. "How long?"

"About the time you took Maddie home."

"That was the first time?" His blue eyes pierce me.

I nod, my hand falling away from my mouth. "Just after."

He laughs bitterly and turns to Aston. "I go away for two days and you jump into bed with her a week later?"

"With each other!" I step forward. "Each. Other, Braden!"

"Oh and that's supposed to make it fucking better is it?"

"No!" I move in front of Aston. "No, it isn't. Nothing can make it better and I have no excuses for this, but you have to realize I can make my own decisions. I'm old enough to deal with the fall-out. I love that you have my back, I do, but you can't always be there to protect me! Aston didn't force me into anything. Do you get that? I *wanted* to!"

His eyes focus on me, my chest heaves, and Aston touches my arm.

"Megs–"

"No," I say, my eyes on Braden. "As much as he'd like to believe it, it's not just you. I'm not gonna stand here and watch him give you shit because of something we both did."

"How long have you been sleeping with *each other*?" Braden says sarcastically. "Because it makes the world of fucking difference."

"*We* have been in a *relationship* since the weekend after you left," I correct him.

"Ha!" Braden slams his hand into the wall. "A relationship? Are you fucking serious?"

"Yes."

"Fucking unreal. You've made some shit choices, Megan, but this tops the goddamn list!" He passes through the door. I wrench my arm from Aston's grip and follow him, not caring who can hear this conversation.

"The decision to be with Aston wasn't the bad choice! The bad one was keeping it from you – and you know why that happened? You know why I didn't tell you? Because of this. To stop this happening! I knew you'd go bat shit crazy over it!"

"So why did you fucking do it?" he throws over his shoulder.

"Because I wanted to!"

"And that makes it better?" He stops, turning to look at me. He motions in the direction of Aston's room. "He's just gonna break your heart, Megan! That's what he does. He fucks girls and leaves them–"

"You don't know him like I do!"

"No, but there's a lot of girls that do!"

"No they don't!" I yell, my foot stamping. My hands come up to the sides of my head. "They don't know him the way I do. None of you do, so don't you fucking stand there and tell me it was a bad decision when you know nothing – *nothing* – about my decision! You know nothing about us. You know *nothing* about how I feel, or how he feels!"

"Go on, then, Megs. If it's such a big thing, the *real fucking deal*, tell me. How do you feel?"

I look at him steadily, opening my mouth to speak.

"I love her," Aston says from halfway down the hall. "I can't answer for her, but I can answer for me. And the answer is I love her."

My hands fall to my sides, and I swallow. My heart takes up a frantic beat in my chest, pounding and rattling against my ribs. We've never said it. He's never said it.

And now he's admitting it. Out loud. To Braden. And anyone else listening.

"Do you love her or what she gives you?" Braden asks uncertainly, his voice still laced with anger.

Aston steps up behind me, reaching down and taking my hands in his. His fingers lace through mine, and as his chest touches mine I can feel the vulnerability in him. The only person he's ever opened up to about anything is me, and now he has to do it to someone else.

"I love her for who she is, and who I am when I'm with her. Everything Maddie does for you, times that by a million, and that's what Megan does for me. She's right, Braden. None of you know me like she does. She knows everything about me – even the things I didn't want anyone to ever know. She knows them and she's still here. I love her for everything she gives me, every touch, every smile, I love it all.

"You can come flying at me now and kick the shit out of me. I'll take it because I deserve it for going behind your back, but I won't fucking apologize. I won't ever apologize for loving her, so don't expect me to. And don't expect me to walk away from her because I won't. I can't."

He tightens his grip on my hands slightly, and my body shakes. Gentle footsteps on the stairs announce Maddie's arrival, and my eyes slide to hers. I don't see the anger or annoyance I expect.

I see understanding.

"And you, Meggy?" Braden questions.

Deep breath. "I love him, Bray. I'm sorry I didn't tell you, I am. Both of us tried not to let it happen but it did, and I'm not sorry for that. I'm just sorry it hurts you so much."

Maddie slides her arm around Braden's, leaning against him, and he heaves out a breath.

"Y'know what hurts the most?" He looks at me, anger gone from his eyes. A hint of defeat replaces it. "You're my best friend and you didn't think you could tell me. You didn't even feel for a second that you could tell me. Maybe that's my fault, but that's what gets me. Am I pissed you lied about it? Fucking right I am. I'm fuming. But I can't be mad at you. No matter how much I want to slam my fist into Aston's face and yell at you, I can't."

"Why not?" Aston asks. "I'd deserve it."

Braden's eyes go over my shoulder to meet the gray pair I love. "Because when I look in Megan's eyes I see the same love for you that Maddie has in hers for me. You didn't hesitate for a second to tell me you love her, when she didn't even know yet. I could tell that from her reaction. You hadn't told her, and I made you tell me. I'd be a fucking hypocrite if I was mad at you for that, but just because I'm not mad doesn't mean I want to be around you right now."

He shakes his arm from Maddie and walks down the stairs to his room. Maddie looks at both of us, a small smile playing on her lips.

"It took long enough for you to admit it," she says softly.

"You knew?" Aston pulls me closer to him.

Her smile grows a little, and she tucks some hair behind her ear. "Of course I did. I know pain, Aston, and pain knows pain. You have some pain deep inside you, I don't know what it is, but I know it's there. And Megs is the softest, most understanding person I know. You two were drawn together because she could heal your wounds. I've known since we got back that you two had something."

"Why didn't you ask me?" I tilt my head to the side slightly.

She makes to follow Braden, pausing on the top stair. "Because …" She grins. "If Braden had any suspicions and asked me if you'd said anything, I wouldn't have had to lie to him."

I can't help but smile. She knows him so well. She knows him like I know Aston.

I breathe out deeply, letting myself relax against him. His arms wrap around me tightly, his face burying into my neck.

"That was … Fun," he says dryly.

"That went well," I say truthfully. "I was expecting Braden to punch first, ask later. That's his usual M.O."

"Maybe he was just so shocked you were actually there that he forgot to punch me first."

I let out a small laugh. "I think that's probably right."

He releases me and steers us back into his room, nudging the door shut. I rub my hands down my face.

"What do we do now?" I look at him.

Aston grins, moving toward me. "We stop hiding, and I get to go all protective on your pretty little ass when some dickhead tries to hit on you."

My lips curve up on one side. He cups my face and brushes his lips across mine.

"That sounds about right."

"Yep. We just have to clear something up first."

"What's that?"

His gray eyes clear, becoming raw and honest. "I'm sorry I never told you how I feel."

"I know now," I respond.

He shakes his head a little. "No, you don't. You don't know how just a touch of your hand can take away the pain from my past, and you don't know how lying next to you at night stops the nightmares. You don't know that you're the first person to really make me smile, and you definitely don't know that I'm so in love with you I can't see or think straight. 'In vain have I struggled. It will not do. My feelings will not be repressed. You must allow me to tell you how ardently I admire and love you.'"

Damn. He gets the British accent perfect. I smile up

at him, and resting my hands on his waist, I move our bodies closer. His fingers slip into my hair, curling around the back of my head, barely brushing the top of my neck.

"Even when I tried not to, I still did," he says in a softer voice, resting his forehead against mine. My nose brushes his, and I close my eyes, just listening to him. "I stepped over the edge and started falling for you, and I'm damn sure I don't ever want to get back up from it. I don't know how you do it, baby, but you make me better."

Aston touches his lips to mine, a feather-light brush, and I slide my hands around and up his back to his shoulders.

"A speech worthy of Mr. Darcy," I mutter, smiling. He pulls his face back, his eyes lighter, his lips curved upwards. My hands move along his arms, and I hold his gaze intensely. "I love you, Aston. I don't know how or why, I just know that I do. Everything you think about yourself, everything you've been told, I see and think the complete opposite. You are worth everything to me – *everything*. Okay? And I promise you here and now, I won't leave."

He takes a shuddery breath, vulnerability flickering in his eyes. Instead of saying anything he dips his face toward mine, and our lips meet again. His hands slide down my back, and as I wrap my arms around his neck our bodies align perfectly.

"You don't have a choice," Aston whispers, his breath fanning across my lips. "Because I don't think I'll ever let you leave. Besides, we never had a proper first kiss."

"We did. Up against a wall after you attacked me, I believe."

"That wasn't a kiss. That was a prelude to sex that never happened."

"Yes, but kissing happened," I remind him.

The corner of his mouth twitches slightly. "But it wasn't a kiss – not a proper kiss."

"You've kissed me hundreds of times, Aston."

"I know. But we still never had a real first kiss."

I sigh, slightly amused by this. "Why is that so important to you?"

"Because you're the most romantic person I know, and I know it matters to you."

"It doesn't matter that much." I gaze into his smoky eyes. "It's just a kiss."

"Nothing with you is 'just' anything," he mutters, smiling. "It's always more than it seems, and I want to give you the first kiss you deserve."

"You don't have to do anything. Having us is more than enough."

"Megan …"

"You're not going to give up on the idea of a second first kiss, are you?"

Aston shakes his head. "I'll never give up on anything where you're concerned. So let me have my way."

"Fine," I whisper.

He dips his face toward me, the tip of his nose brushing mine. My eyes flutter closed.

"I hope you're ready for the best first kiss of your

life," he whispers. "Because it's gonna be your last first kiss."

His hand slides to the back of my head and pushes us together. Our mouths meet, a soft touch that becomes gently more probing. His lips caress mine slowly, and my body sinks into him. The taste of him, the feel of him, the smell of him – it all takes me over. With each brush of his lips I feel myself falling deeper into him, even deeper than I am already.

I feel myself crashing into him with everything I have, crashing into him and holding on tightly to everything he has to give. Because the romantic in me wants it all and it won't let it go. At all.

~

My heart is in complete contradiction of itself. Lying here in Aston's arms, half of it is lighter than it's been in the last few weeks. The lightness comes from the truth being told. But the other half is heavy, like a lead weight is holding it down and pinning it to the ground.

I shift, and Aston's grip on me tightens. I run my fingers through his hair, smoothing it back from his face, and study him. Now he looks like he's at peace. The lines on his forehead I've seen so many times are now completely smooth, his mouth is slightly open, and his breathing is even and steady.

But his peace has come at the torment of my best friend – who's somewhere in this house, probably awake.

He'll be hating himself for being mad at me, happy I found the love he has, and guilty I felt like I couldn't tell him.

In fact he won't be at the house. I know exactly where he'll be.

I climb out of bed, and there's a light knock at the door. Crap. I grab one of Aston's shirts from the back of his chair, throw it over my head and open the door a crack. Lila's face stares back at me.

"I ran back to the dorm room to get you some clothes. I knew you didn't have any and you'd be up now." She holds out a bag.

"Thank you," I say quietly.

"Hey – you don't need to thank me. I don't wanna be you today. Braden isn't even here; he left Maddie a note on her cell that he needed an hour. She gets it but has no idea where he is."

"That's why you got me clothes."

She laughs into her hand. "Partly. I know it's no good all of us going and searching for him – I mean, he could be anywhere, right? You're the one person who will find him."

I nod. "I know where he'll be. Tell Mads not to worry; I'll find him. Thanks for bringing this, Li."

She smiles and walks down the hall to Ryan's room. I close the door behind me and turn to see Aston's gray eyes staring at me hotly. I ignore the feeling that sweeps my body and hold up the bag.

"Lila got me clothes."

"If I didn't just hear that Braden's disappeared and

you're the only person who knows where he is, I'd go and give those damn clothes back to her." He props himself up on his elbow, his eyes locked to the top of my thighs where the hem of his shirt falls.

"You would?" I ask innocently, walking over to the bed.

"Fucking right I would." He grabs my arm and pulls me toward him. I land half on him, half on the bed, and his hands creep beneath the shirt, his fingers tracing inside the line of my panties. "I would absolutely say you should sleep in my shirt, but there's a slim chance of any sleep actually happening if you did."

"I don't think I would complain," I say against his mouth, brushing lips with him.

He kisses me hard, and at a shift of his hips his erection pushes into my bare thigh through the covers. I run my fingers through his hair and break the kiss, grinning down at him.

"I need to go find Bray."

"I know," he replies softly. "It's not fair on Maddie either now. Shit. We've made a mess of this, haven't we?"

I sit up, running my fingertips down his arm to the palm of his hand. He catches my fingers with his, linking them together.

"Yeah. We have. There's no point lying about it, but honestly, regardless of when we told him it would have happened. He still would have been angry and needed to cool off. We know we shouldn't have kept us a secret and we should have told him a long time ago, but there's nothing we can do about that now. It was wrong, and now I need to go and speak to him and make it right."

"He's a stubborn ass. How do you know he'll talk to you?"

I smile, shrugging one shoulder. "Because if he wanted to talk to anyone else, he wouldn't have gone to where only I would know where to look for him."

~

"I wondered how long it would take you."

The wind coming in off the bay whips my hair around my face, leaving me to battle it constantly. "Longer than it should have," I respond, hopping up onto the rock next to Braden. I shove my hair from my face again.

He says nothing and shrugs his shoulders, looking out across the choppy water. His thumbs flick against each other, his feet tapping to an invisible beat. I know him well enough to know he's thinking about what to say, so I keep quiet, waiting for him to make the first move.

"I understand why you did it," he says after a moment of silence. "I mean, why you kept it secret. I don't understand why you'd sleep with that ass."

I glance at him and catch the twitching of his lips. "Umm … He's hot?" I offer, trying not to grin. Turning his face away, Braden bites the inside of his cheek. I look down.

"Yeah, well, I guess if you have to be with some fucker, it should be a fucker I actually like."

"You'll never like anyone I date." I rest my head on his shoulder, and he puts his arms round mine the way we used to whenever we chatted. Before we left for college. Before games started.

"True," he agrees. "But I can't completely hate Aston because I liked him before, so I'm fucked. Although I gotta admit I never imagined you with him. I imagined you with some rich bastard driving a soft top car, spending your days racing down the interstates between L.A. and New York for fancy dinners."

Laughter explodes from me, and I cover my mouth as Braden shakes next to me, laughing himself.

"Right – because I absolutely have the manners and patience for that, don't I? Puh-lease, Bray, give me some credit." I nudge his side, still giggling slightly. "And have you forgotten your mom's charity do thing? We had to Google which fork to use because no one told us the proper etiquette. They all assumed two fourteen year olds knew that sort of thing."

"And when we came here I had to Google dating," he muses. "Damn. We drew some short straws, didn't we?"

"I think it's because you were always in trouble, so by default I was too." I smile and sit up slightly. "I really am sorry, Bray. I never wanted to keep it from you. It was just supposed to be once and everything kind of snowballed, then before I knew it, it was too far to do anything. The longer I left it the harder it got to find the words to tell you. It makes me a total shit, and believe me when I say I feel like an utter bitch because I do. It's hurt you so much."

"I get it, Megs. Sorta. It makes me feel like shit you couldn't tell me, but I'd probably have done the same if I was you. But I wouldn't have gotten caught." He grins.

"I wanted to get caught." I shrug. "At least I think I did. If you caught us I wouldn't have had to come out and explain it because you would have guessed."

"You always were the wimp."

"Hey!"

"Aston is a jackass, Megs, I know that. But he loves you. I didn't think it was fucking possible, but he does." He pauses for a moment. "Then again this is you. You could turn a gay guy straight if you really wanted to."

"Well . . . I bet I could give it a good go."

"Good luck. Aston will kick his ass, gay or not. If he's anything like me he will."

"When it comes to being an overprotective asswipe? Yep, pretty much exactly the same."

Braden laughs slightly, then sighs. "I'm sorry, too, Meggy."

"What for? I'm the one who lied."

He turns his face toward mine, blue eyes meeting blue eyes. "Because I was so wrapped up in what I thought was best for you I forgot to stop and ask what *you* wanted. I was so fuckin' set on keeping you away from any of the walking, talking dicks in the frat house I didn't realize the best thing for you was right under my damn nose the whole time."

"He never made it easy." My voice softens slightly. "Part of the reason I never told you was because he might not say it but he needs you and Ry. He needs the banter and friendship you provide him. It gives him security. I meant what I said when I said you don't know him like I do. It's not for me to tell you – I won't betray him that way – but the guy you know isn't the one I know. You just have to trust me when I say he's what's best. You know the heart doesn't lie, Bray, and my heart tells me he's what's best for me. My heart tells me he's all I'm ever gonna need, no matter how hard it gets."

"And that's why I can't be mad. No matter how much I want to be. I trust you, girl. Sometimes I have to ask myself why, but it's no damn good arguing with your stubborn ass."

"You taught me well."

"Too fucking well." He stretches and stands up, putting his hands on my waist and hoisting me up. He slings his arm over my shoulders. "Come on, then. I ran out on my girlfriend this morning and I have to go threaten some pretty-boy ass."

I shake my head as we jump from the rock, smiling. No good fighting it.

He still needs to be macho-man big bro.

Chapter Twenty-Two - Aston

The rough bark of the tree digs into my back. Apart from with Megan, outside is the only place that gives me peace. Even as I wait for the inevitable conversation with Braden – the one where I'll have to admit why I need her so much. He deserves that much after what we've done to him, and I'm ready for it. Because of Megan I'm finally ready to start opening up about my life.

"Still a spacey bastard." He smirks.

"No fist in my eye?" I smirk back at him.

He shrugs a shoulder. "I considered it. Several fucking times. Then figured it just ain't worth it since I'd probably get more punches from those damn girls than it's worth."

He's probably right.

"But that doesn't mean I won't kick the shit out of you if you break her fucking heart."

"I wasn't joking when I said I loved her yesterday," I say bluntly, staring him down with the same seriousness he's looking at me with. "She gets me, man. She gets all my shit and she deals with it. She's something out of this damn world, and I still think I don't deserve her."

"Dude, none of us deserve these girls, but for some reason they won't leave us alone." He winks. "I ain't gonna lie to you – I'm pissed. I'm pissed you never told me and that you went behind my back to do it all. But at the same time I get it, yeah? You kept that fuckin' secret because of how much she means to me… That's why I'm not completely pissed."

I raise my eyebrows at him, questioning him silently. He opens his mouth and closes it again.

"Fuck it." He runs his hand through his hair. "I don't even know what I am."

Megan appears at the back door of the frat house and leans against the doorframe and watches us.

"Until I was six, my life was a mess of drugs, alcohol, sex and abuse. I spent my time hiding the bruises my mom's jacked-up boyfriends gave me and wondering what they'd get me for next time. I listened to her being used in the next room. I listened to her sobbing and crying every night. I watched her go too far until eventually the drugs killed her and my Gramps took me in. I've lived with that bullshit ever since, and I used sex to block it all out the same way she did. That was why I never gave a fuck. Sex meant I didn't have to feel – until Megan. She made it all real again. She reminded me of how I feel about everything, and slowly she pulled it all out of me. She made me relive all the memories and then she took it all away by just being there. The shit in my head, all that noise, she makes it quiet again, man. I'm fucked if I know how she does it." I shake my head, watching as she makes her way over to us slowly. "But she does. That's the shit no one else knows." My eyes fall back on Braden's. "That's the real me, and the least I can do after betraying you this way is tell you the kind of person she's in love with. I'm not gonna pretend anymore. I'm just gonna be fucking real because that's what Megan deserves."

"You haven't ended up killing each other yet then?" Megan tucks some hair behind her ear and stops right between us. I reach forward and grab her hand, pulling her down. She squeals, and I catch her and gently make her sit between my legs. My arms tuck around her waist and I nuzzle the side of her head, kissing the spot below her ear.

"No, no killing. Another few minutes and it might have been a possibility."

She turns her face toward me, and I feel the twitch of her cheek as she smiles. Her fingers link through mine.

"Good," she mutters. "I'd hate to have to deal with both of you."

"See?" Braden shrugs. "She could kick my ass better than I could kick yours. At least I'm here to keep an eye on you, I guess. Make sure you treat her right."

"Caveman," Maddie reminds him, dropping onto the grass next to him.

"Whatever, Angel. I'm just saying."

"We know." She leans over and kisses his cheek. "But I think Aston is aware of that."

Braden grunts, and Maddie smiles, resting her head on his shoulder.

"This is the jackass you've been sleeping with?" Kay hollers across the yard. "Are you fucking kidding me?"

"Uh, surprise?" Megan says weakly and shrugs.

"Surprise? Damn right it's a fuckin' surprise!" She stops, towering over us, and puts her hands on her hips.

She looks at Braden. "Why isn't his whole body in plaster?"

Braden shrugs. I'm pretty sure everyone shrugs around Kay. It's easier to do that than answer her and give her more ammunition to vomit words.

"Chill out, Bitchy-Pants!" Lila calls. "They're just dating. No biggie."

"You knew, didn't you?" Kay rounds on her, then on Megan. "How could you tell her and not me?"

I smirk as Megan looks at her pointedly.

"Technically, she didn't tell me," Lila mentions. "I worked it out."

"Why didn't you tell me?"

"Was it a matter of life and death, Kayleigh? Will you drop down dead now you're the last person to find out?"

"No."

"Then that's why I didn't tell you." Lila grins. "None of your business."

"You knew?" Braden asks Lila, glancing over her shoulder to Ryan. "Did you know?"

"Why do I feel like we're in the middle of a high school drama?" I whisper in Megan's ear. She giggles silently.

"Because Kay, Braden, and Ryan are still of high school mentality?" she whispers back.

"I, er, shit," Lila mutters.

"Don't look at me, man. It's news to me that Lila knew."

"News … Knew … News …" Maddie blinks a few times. "Um, can I just summarize here? My head is starting to hurt."

"That'll be the shots you threw back last night," Kay remarks.

"Nope. It's definitely from you guys." Maddie shakes her head. "Okay, Megan and Aston had a saucy one-nighter, leaving them dying and in desperate need of each other's company. This resulted in them starting and maintaining a secret relationship while Megan continued to fake-date guys Lila pre-approved and set her up with to keep up the facade. She then had enough, told Lila where to stick her blind dates, and spilled the beans. Then Lila covered for her until last night when they had enough, got sloppy, and Braden caught them. Now we all know, everyone is happy, and they can have unlimited one-nighters, therefore never needing to worry about being caught with their pants round their ankles while bumping uglies against a tree."

Megan snorts. I grin.

"We have never had sex up against a tree," she mumbles.

"Hey, not yet . . ." I squeeze her waist.

"Is that it, though?" Maddie looks at us. "Well, basically."

"Um, I guess so . . . Kinda elaborate, but yeah." Megan answers for us. "Maybe a little less desperation, though."

"I'm not sure. I've been pretty desperate to get inside your pants since I saw you," I tell her.

"Just my pants?"

"Well, we could go for inside you, but I was trying not to be fucking crude about it."

Her eyes twinkle.

"Okay, usually I'd be totally up for sex talk, but the girl is like my sister. No next morning fuck stories." Braden puts his hands up and looks at me. "Try and keep that shit to a minimum around me."

"You know," Maddie muses. "Aston doesn't swear nearly as much since him and Megan did the nasty. Maybe you should try it, Bray." She taps his cheek, and he rolls his eyes.

"Of course, Angel," he deadpans.

I smirk.

"I can't believe you were fucking each other and I never figured it out." Kay looks at us.

"Relationship," Megan corrects. "There's a difference."

"Sex was involved. It's all relative. I just can't believe I didn't know."

I resist the urge to roll my eyes. "You're not going to shut up about it, are you?"

"No," Kay replies, leaning back on her hands. "It's not damn likely."

~

"What are we doing?" I ask as Megan tugs me toward my car.

"It's Sunday," she says simply. "We're going to see

your Gramps."

"Okay, but that doesn't explain why you have a damn picnic basket with you."

"Fine – we're going to see your Gramps and take him out for the day. Better?" She raises an eyebrow at me, and I grin, starting the engine up.

"Much. But where are we going?"

"You'll see."

She settles back in her seat, smiling to herself. If I'd hoped to get any clues from her outfit, I've definitely not got any luck. Her jeans, jacket, and boots are nothing out of the ordinary – but her tied up hair is.

Not that it means anything in particular … Apart from making me want to nuzzle her bare neck.

We pull up outside Gramps' house and get out. When I open the door, I'm not greeted by the usual smell of cigar smoke. It's there, but fainter.

"Gramps?" I call out, worry trickling its way through my body. Worry shoots through my veins at a lightning speed when I see his empty chair by the window. He always sits by the window. Where is he?

"Gramps!" I shout loudly, spinning around and heading for the stairs. "Gramps!"

"You could wake the damn dead you could, boy," his voice grumbles from the back door. I rush through the kitchen and find him wiping dirt off his hands.

I stop. "You were gardening?"

"No need to sound so surprised." He chuckles. "It's been known to happen."

"But you haven't done it for years."

"That's because I got lazy, boy!" He drops the cloth on the counter. "I planted them bushes I got a couple weeks back – the hydrangea ones. For your Gran."

"I thought you weren't ready to," I say softly.

"I wasn't! Then me and you had our little chat, and I thought to myself what a miserable old bastard I was. Decided to get out of that damn chair and do something about it. You should go take a look at that vegetable garden. Not much growing there right now, but by spring it'll be bloomin'!" He beams, a light in his face I haven't seen for so long. He glances over my shoulder and his face brightens even more. "And you brought Megan! Well, gardening and a chat about books with a beautiful young lady. This is the best Sunday I've had in a while."

Megan laughs softly. "I was hoping you'd be out of that chair. I'm taking you out for the day."

I clear my throat, amused. "Who's taking who?"

"Okay so you're driving, but it's most definitely my treat, Mr. Banks." She looks at me pointedly, humor dancing in her pretty blue eyes.

"And the beautiful lady wants to take me out?" Gramps rubs his hands together. "I best get my coat. Aston, I'm stealing your girl!" He kisses Megan on the side of the head as he passes her, a bounce in his step.

"Not a chance, old man!"

Megan smiles fondly at him, and I walk across the room to her, stopping in front of her.

"Yes?" She looks up at me.

I cup her chin, running my thumb along her jaw to her bottom lip. I trace it softly. "Nothing." I smile, tilting her chin up and bending my face to meet her lips.

"Hope you're not seducing my girl!" Gramps calls. "We have a date to go on!"

I laugh, taking Megan's hand and leading her out the house. Gramps grabs his stick and points it at the car.

"Least that beast is clean."

"Of course it's clean. You really think I'd let her get dirty?" I glance at him.

He grunts. "No. Guess not."

I grin, helping him into the car, and shut the door. I get in the front next to Megan and she's smiling to herself.

"Gonna tell me where we're going yet?"

She shakes her head, eyes twinkling. "No. I'll just give you directions. It's a surprise. Go right at the end of the street."

I sneak glances at her as I drive and make the turns she orders me to. I'm not really paying attention to the direction we're going in. I'm too preoccupied by the excitement she's showing. It's infectious – I'm excited and I don't even know what for.

"Marina," Gramps says from the back seat. "We're heading to the marina."

Megan grins and turns in her seat, nodding her head. "Yep."

"Why?" I frown slightly and glance at Gramps in the back seat. He taps a wrinkled finger against his mouth as he thinks, and Megan's grin grows.

"Why do people usually go to the marina?" she asks.

"Boats," I answer. Her eyes slide to mine, her excitement really obvious now. Her cheeks are flushed, but behind the light in her eyes there's a hint of nervousness. Why …

"Fishing!" Gramps cries. "You're taking us fishing!"

Megan nods vigorously. "I wanted to do something for you both. My parents were supposed to come this weekend but Dad had a work thing come up so they canceled. He had a boat booked to go out with Braden, so I asked if I could use it instead. I'm paying him back."

I stop the car in the parking lot near the marina and turn around to see Gramps. His eyes glisten with unshed tears, and a lump rises in my own throat.

"Thank you," he whispers to Megan, his eyes focused on hers. "Thank you." She smiles in response, and Gramps shakes his head. "I'm gonna go to that fishing place over the road and get us some bait. Megan, do you fish?"

She shakes her head. "God, no. My dad taught Braden to fish, and his mom taught me to shop." She grins. "It worked out well."

"Then make sure they have three poles on that boat," Gramps announces. "We'll teach you to fish!"

"Oh, I, er, um …"

"Nope! You're coming on that boat, so you're fishing. No just sitting there and looking pretty. You can look pretty and fish at the same time, you know." He winks and opens the car door.

"Hang on, Gramps."

"I can get out of a car, boy. I'm not that old yet," he scolds me, grabbing his stick and climbing out. "I'm getting bait. You go and sort out that boat."

He hobbles across the street with his stick. I open Megan's door for her, pull her out, and close to me. Her arms go round my waist and she leans her cheek against my chest.

"Thank you," I whisper, kissing the top of her head, letting my lips linger there. "Thank you for this. You don't know how much it means to him."

She pulls her head back and half-smiles. "Probably about as much as it means to you."

I nod, realizing it's true. "We haven't fished since before the semester started."

She runs her hands around to my stomach, her fingers splaying as they creep up my chest to my neck. "I don't have to stay, you know. It's your day. You and your Gramps can go out by yourselves if you–"

I silence her with a kiss. "No. No. Fishing was always our thing, just me and him, but if there was anyone in this world I want to share it with, it's you." And it's true. She's the only person I'd dream of sharing this with.

"Then let's get to that boat. I bet he's lethal with that stick, let alone fishing poles."

~

The waters of the bay are calm today, and the small boat bobs along smoothly. Megan's picnic is out of the way of any splashing water and she's looking dubiously at the fishing poles. Her gaze drifts to the tubs of worms Gramps bought for bait and she scrunches her face up a little. I can't help but smile.

"They're just worms," I comment as I casually hook one onto my pole.

"Exactly," she mutters, still staring the tub down. "*Worms.* If I'd have known we'd be using real live worms, I . . ." She shudders. "I hate worms."

I smirk. "They're just worms, baby. You need them to hook the fish."

"I know that." She finally looks up at me. "I just wish I didn't *have* to need them."

Gramps hands her a pole. "You need to hook the bait."

She takes a deep breath as I hold the tub out, trying to contain my amusement. Her fingers move toward the tub before she snatches her hand back, shuddering again.

It takes her five tries to grab one. Even then, she drops it.

"Grab the damn worm and slide that hook through it!" Gramps claps his hands. "Those fish ain't gonna wait around all day to become someone's dinner!"

"I . . . *Ewwww*!" she squeals as she grabs one quickly and slides it on. She holds the pole away from her body, the hooked worm floating through the air , and wipes her fingers on a rag next to her. "Ew, ew, ew, ew!"

I secure the lid on the tub and Gramps and I burst into laughter.

"Come on. We gotta catch some fish!" Gramps grabs his pole, hooks his bait, and casts out onto the water.

"Yeah . . ." Megan says vaguely. "I have no freakin' idea how that works."

I put my pole down and pull her up. "I'll teach you."

"He learned from the best!" Gramps calls from the other side of the boat.

I wink at Megan and position her in front of me, wrapping one of my arms around her stomach. "The wind is blowing from behind us, so we need to cast this way. If we try to go against it, it'll just blow your line this way."

"Right. But how do I cast it?"

I grin. "Patience. You need to hold the rod correctly."

"Um, sure."

I move my hand from her stomach and wrap my fingers around hers. "The reel needs to be facing down, and it should sit between your middle finger and ring finger for balance. Like this." I move her fingers. "If that isn't comfy, you can change it until it is."

"Its fine," she says a little breathlessly.

"Now . . ." I move my mouth closer to her ear. "You need to reel out until you have six inches of line hanging out, and turn the handle until the roller is directly under your middle finger." I help her do it, my fingertips brushing against hers. "Now hold the line against the rod, and open the bait with your other hand."

I take her free hand from the side of the boat and put it against the bait, opening it with her.

"Now what?" She leans back into me slightly.

"Point the rod at your target." I help her position it. "Now we need to bring it up in a smooth, swift motion. You'll feel when the top of the rod bends and as soon as it does, we need to push it forward. Halfway to the target, let go of the line. Then we'll close the bait."

"Up, bend, forward, let go, close," she mutters, leaning back into me. "I think I can do that."

"You can." I run my lips along her ear, nibbling at her lobe slightly. She wriggles and draws in a sharp breath.

"I can't if you do that."

I smile against her skin. "Ready to try."

"No."

"Three, two, one." I help her lift the rod straight up and when I feel the flex I flick it forwards. She squeaks. "Let go!"

Megan lifts her finger from the line and it flies out with rod, landing almost perfectly in the water. She grins. "I did it!"

"You did. Now you have to wait for a fish to bite."

"How long does that take?"

"How long is a piece of string?"

Chapter Twenty-Three - Megan

"Are you telling me I could be standing here all day and not catch a thing?"

Gramps cackles across the boat. "That's exactly what he's telling you!"

I turn my face toward Aston, and he grins. "What?"

"I can't believe I got roped into this." This is ridiculous. I eat fish. I don't catch it. Hell.

"Hey." His hands fall to my hips and he nudges my collar from my neck with his nose. His lips brush the skin of my neck. "This was your idea, remember?"

"Yes . . ." My idea for them.

Aston's nose runs up and down my neck, his breath hot against me, and I swallow.

"So you didn't get roped into anything. You had to know that you'd end up fishing," he reasons.

"Mhmm."

"So why are you so surprised?"

I shiver when he takes a deep breath and exhales against my skin. His hands slide down my sides to the front pockets of my jeans. He puts his fingers in them, spreading them out and stroking my legs, before taking them back out.

"I'm not," I whisper.

"Then don't complain." He's smiling as he brushes his lips along my jaw lightly, and my eyelids flutter shut.

Shit. He's driving me insane. "Megan," he whispers in my ear.

"Mm?"

"Keep your eyes on the line."

Bastard. My eyes snap open and I look at him. The desire in his eyes is probably equal to what's in mine, and fuck this stupid boat. Why do we have to be on a boat? "You did that deliberately."

He bends his head round and steals a kiss. He grins. "So what if I did?"

I narrow my eyes and look back out at the water. "So not–"

"Woohooooooo!" Gramps hollers. "We've got a big one, boy!"

"Hold that steady," Aston tells me, releasing me and making his way across the boat to his Gramps, grabbing a net on the way.

"Giz a hand, here. Not as steady on the old feet as I used to be," Gramps orders him. I glance over my shoulder and watch as Aston grabs the pole. It's bending a hella lot, and he whistles low at it.

"That's a good one, Gramps."

"Don't sound so surprised," he grunts. "Prize fisher, me."

He reels in the fish slowly, and as soon as it nears the surface, Aston swoops it up with the net and drops it onto the boat.

"Late salmon!" Gramps cries happily, taking a seat and bending over to look at it. "And … You got a tape measure on you?"

"In the picnic bag," I answer. "Dad always used to take one for Braden so I thought I'd pack it."

"Genius, girl!"

I grin, and Aston leaves the fish flapping on the deck to grab the tape measure.

"Well, is it big enough?"

"I think . . ." He rolls it out next to the fish. "Hold him still, Gramps." He rests his foot on the slippery salmon as they double-check the length.

"Well?"

"Just." Aston grins at Gramps. "Half an inch over the size limit."

He claps his hands. "Dinner tonight, kids!"

Something tugs on my line and my whole body twitches. I stare at the rod and the rapidly increasing line.

"Oh!" I squeak. "Something is there! What do I do? Help!"

Gramps winks, grabs a stick and kills the fish quickly. Aston steps back up behind me and steadies my hands on the rod.

"There's a fish – has it bitten?" he asks me.

"How am I supposed to know? I can't see it!"

He half-sighs, half-laughs, and rests the side of his head against mine. "This is gonna be a long day."

~

So I'm not cut out to be a fisherwoman.

That's fine. I'm not particularly fond of the worms anyway … Or the shrimps. Worms are meant for gardens, and shrimps are made for eating. If you wanna catch 'em or fish with 'em, that's cool. I just won't do it.

Although I might just be tempted if Aston pressed himself up against me the way he did today …

Even in the cold sea breeze, I still felt like my body was on fire when he was behind me. I was so aware of him and the slightest movement of his body I don't think I actually learned a freaking thing about fishing. All I could think about was his fingers playing with my jeans pockets and his lips ghosting along my neck. Add in the warmth of his breath across my goose pimple covered skin, and I'm ready to melt against him right now at the mere thought.

Now back in his room after eating the salmon, Aston's hands ease up my thighs and his thumbs brush along the inner side. I look into his gray eyes as he leans into me and runs his nose down mine.

"You didn't need to do that today," he mutters as his fingers probe their way to my ass.

"I know, but I wanted to. You guys loved it."

"It was made better by you being there." His nose nudges at my jaw, causing my head to tilt back.

"You were pressed up against my body for most of it." I run my fingers through his hair, and he presses open-mouth kisses along my shoulder. "I'm sure it was better than normal."

"It was. Much better."

He dips his tongue in the hollow of my collarbone,

my shirt catching as he moves his hands up my back. I turn my head and kiss his neck, resting my cheek against his shoulder. He breathes out heavily, shuddering slightly, and I recognize that movement. He's remembering. I hold him tighter and press my face into him.

"You don't have to leave, do you?" His voice is small and vulnerable, cutting into my chest.

"No," I whisper. "I'll stay as long as you need me to."

And I mean it. If he needed me to stay forever, right here in his arms, I would. I'll stay for as long as he needs me whenever he needs me.

"Good."

His fingers dig into my back and his jaw clenches, his whole body going rigid. I slowly smooth my hands across his back, slipping them under his shirt. His muscles are solid beneath my fingers, rock solid, and his grip on me tightens as he tries to control the shaking of his hands through shallow breaths.

I feel the burn of tears as I sit here, completely powerless to stop whatever is going through his mind. He could be remembering anything, any horror, and there's no way I can stop it. I've been here so many times already and it's ripped my heart apart each and every time.

But I won't leave. Love is stronger than hate.

Whatever hate is locked inside his body and whatever hate is burned into his mind, I know our love can push it out. I believe in the power it gives us.

And that's why I will break my heart over and over again.

I will break my heart to heal his.

"Don't go." The words are a muffled, desperate plea into my hair.

"I'm not going anywhere," I promise him. "I'm right here. I'll be here as long as you need me."

"I hate . . ."

"You're safe." My voice is soft yet firm, my hand moving to the back of his head as I fight through the tears threatening to spill from my eyes. "You're safe here with me."

His body twitches and he relaxes suddenly, his breathing broken and harsh. "Megan."

Shit. He's so broken. His voice is so quiet, so scared. My hands are shaking and my chest is heaving. I'm still fighting the tears that surface every time he remembers.

"I'm here. I'm always here," I reassure him.

"Don't go. Please don't ever go." His voice is ever smaller now, barely there, yet it seems like he's screaming. I feel each word slicing into me, and a tear escapes my eye despite my best efforts.

"I'm staying. I promise. I'm not going anywhere." I stroke the back of his head.

"I remember. Fishing with Gramps and Gran. I was four – it was just before she died. It's patchy. One of the last of her. She was wrapped in her favorite blanket on the boat. Gramps didn't want her to go and she told him to shut up. She wasn't going to miss it. She loved coming on the boat. She's the only person that ever came with us."

Apart from me. His gramps accepted me so readily.

Let me go on a trip that was reserved for them only – and his wife before she died. Today must have meant so much more to them than I thought. I hold that thought and squeeze my eyes shut.

"But then I went home. Took a fish. Mom was there. When Gramps left, she told me to put the fish in the freezer because she had to go to work, and I'd have to have toast because that was all she had. She went to work. I dropped the toast she'd made, the plate smashed, and he was angry. He was so fucking angry. He grabbed me by the back of my tee shirt and shoved me into the wall. My face smacked into it. The bastard broke my nose. Over a fucking plate!"

He tries to push away from me, and I hold him tighter.

"Megs–"

"No."

He rips his head from my grip and stares at me, his eyes hard and cold. I wrap my legs around his, pinning him to me, and cup his face.

"I'm not letting you go," I warn.

"I'm not fucking asking you, Megan!"

"I'm not asking you, either. I'm here, Aston. I'm right here in front of you."

"I . . ."

And I realize. He's scared. He's scared of being the man he was told he would be. Scared of doing the things they did to him to me.

"You're not him! Any of them. You're more than that.

You're *not* them," I finish softly. "You. Are. Not. Them."

"You … I … *Don't*."

"I love you."

He closes his eyes tightly, breathing harshly through his nose, and shakes his head.

"Yes. I love you. Every broken, mismatched piece of you. I love every single freaking piece of you, even when you feel this way, and that isn't gonna change. You can be angry, afraid, sad, and I'll still love you the same way I love you when you're happy. Listen to me and believe me, Aston. I love every part of you the way you love every part of me."

His arms shoot around my waist, and he lies me down on the bed, tucking me into his chest and locking our legs together. His body shakes as he holds me against him. I tilt my head back and stroke my thumb down his jaw and brush his lips. My fingers smooth over his closed eyes, and I press my lips against his softly.

"I'm here, Aston, and I'm not leaving you. Don't push me away anymore. We're past that now. I know all of you and you can't change that."

"I'm scared that one day … One day I will be the person they tried to make me. Don't you get that? I'm scared … I'll hurt you one day. I'm so fucking scared."

"You won't."

His eyes shoot open, locking onto mine with a desperation for answers. "You don't know that."

I do know. I know with every part of me.

"You love me," I say simply. "You have what they

didn't. You have love. *We* have love. Every time you feel that hate, think of me, and I'll give you love. Always."

He doesn't move, his eyes never flickering away, his grip never wavering. The only movement in his body is the rising and falling of his chest as he regains control of his breathing. I run my thumb under his eye and across his cheek again, as if I can wipe away the pain he feels. Like if I do it enough it'll actually work.

A long, pain-filled breath leaves between his lips, and he presses his face to mine, his eyes clearing.

"And this is why I need you," he whispers. "It could be pitch black and you'd still break through with your light."

"You need my love, not me. I'm just the person that gives it to you. I might be your light, but unless you wanted me to, no matter how hard I tried, I wouldn't be able to break through the darkness. You're the one that makes it better. I just help."

He shakes his head, and I nod.

"I give you the light. It's up to you whether or not you let it break through."

"It doesn't make sense."

"What doesn't?"

"Why you love me."

"There's no logic to love. It just is. Just like us. We just are."

~

Everything is easier when a secret is out. Now I don't have to worry about looking at Aston wrong or saying something that might look suspicious. I don't have to watch my every movement, bite my tongue or clench my fists so I don't touch him.

And I love it.

I love that we can just be.

I don't care about the whispers from people outside our circle of friends, the ones who don't know the truth, and I don't care about the looks that come from other girls. I just care that I can fall into his arms when I find him standing outside my classroom, just like he is now.

"Shakespeare hasn't killed you yet, then," he says as he smiles at me, taking my hand.

I look over at him. "No, not yet, but there's every possibility of it in the future."

"Not a damn chance."

"How do you know? Have you ever read act after act of Shakespeare?"

"Because I'd revive you before you completely died."

"And just how would you do that?"

He tugs me out the door and catches me against his body. "A bit like this." He grins and presses his lips to mine hotly, capturing me in a kiss that would most definitely revive me if I was dying.

Hell, I think it would revive me if I was freakin' *dead.*

"Think that would work?" he mutters, a smug grin on his face.

"Yup," I mutter back, slightly dazed.

He laughs, keeping his arm locked around my waist, and steers me in the direction of Starbucks. I snuggle into his side, sighing happily. It's strange to think that a month ago we were constantly bickering, whether it was real or fake, genuine or pretense. Everything has changed so quickly.

We order coffee and take a seat by the window.

"I guess you'll be going home this weekend. For Thanksgiving?"

I look at him and shrug. "I guess so."

"You don't sound happy about it."

I'm not.

"I guess it's the thought of having my mom looking over my shoulder every five minutes. I've had freedom for the last three months. Plus we usually do a thing with Braden's family, but he won't be there this year." I stir my coffee. "I'm pretty sure it's gonna suck without him."

"He isn't going home?"

I shake my head. "He's taking Maddie back to Brooklyn. She doesn't know yet. She thinks they're going to his parents'."

Aston smirks. "He's sneaky."

"He always has been." I smile. "But his sneakiness means I have to suffer through dinner alone." I sigh. Nothing is more tiring than the manners my mother insists on.

"Sounds like fun."

"You could always come suffer with me, you know,"

I offer. "Mom would love that." Once I've told her about us.

"I dunno." He pauses, taking my hand. "I don't wanna leave Gramps alone."

"You don't have to. My nan will be there, and she's about as normal as a straight-sided circle. They'd get along like a house on fire. She'd probably talk him into going to Bingo with her on the Friday night. *And* she smokes like a train." I roll my eyes.

"Perfect match," he says dryly. "And your Granddad?"

"He died in the Vietnam War. He was in the air force and got shot down. I never knew him so it's kinda hard to be sad about it. My other grandparents – Dad's parents – moved to Canada when they retired."

"Canada?" Aston raises an eyebrow. "Isn't that kind of an odd place to retire to?" A small smile creeps onto his face.

"Yes … But I never said they were normal." I grin. "I thought they might have gone to, oh, I dunno, the Bahamas or something. Even moved from Colorado to Cali to be closer to Dad since he moved here to be with Mom after college, but nope. They went to freaking Canada, and we're expected to pack up and go there every winter." I shiver. "It's so damn cold in Canada."

"You really are a Cali princess." He laughs.

"So I grew up in SoCal. Don't shoot me for liking the sun."

"You definitely grew up on the right side of California."

"That's why you and your Gramps should come with. He can go into cahoots with Nan and cause trouble, Mom can entertain the way she loves so much, and me and you can disappear the whole weekend." I shrug. "Sounds good to me."

"I dunno. I'll have to talk to Gramps."

"What would you normally do?"

"Uh ..." Aston scratches the back of his neck, and my lips twitch in amusement. "Eat take-out, watch crap television, and drink beer."

Typical guys. I giggle. "Okay, you're definitely coming with me."

~

"That was traumatic." I drop onto the sofa next to Braden, shaking my head. He grins, and I know exactly what he's about to say.

"She took it well, then?"

"You could say that," I deadpan. "'You have a *boyfriend*? A real boyfriend? Oh, Megan, that's wonderful! Although, I do hope you're using protection. We've had this discussion before, and you need an education, house, and job before you get yourself pregnant.'" I shake my head as if it'll clear the headache brought on by my mom's speech.

"She just cares."

"Oh, I know. I love that she cares so much, but there's really no need to bring it up in every conversation we have. We only spoke ten or so days ago. I'm not that forgetful."

"She means well."

"Yeah?" I raise an eyebrow at him. "Then why can't you stop laughing?"

He shrugs and tries to stop. "I'm sorry, Meggy. I'm just secretly wishing I could see this meet the parents episode."

"Oh, it's meet the grandparents, too. Not doing anything by half."

"Start as you mean to go on." He grins. "Oh, man. I'm gonna have to call Mom three time a day for updates. How much are we betting your mom sits Aston down and gives him the pregnancy chat?"

My eyes widen and I look at him in panic. "She wouldn't."

Braden grins widely, amusement dancing in his eyes. "Oh, I can almost guarantee she will."

I grab a pillow, bury my face into it, and groan. "This is going to be a disaster."

Chapter Twenty-Four - Aston

"This is going to be a disaster," Megan mutters, pulling onto a street with houses worth more than I could ever dream of making. Most are three-story buildings, all with driveways, garages and perfectly pruned front yards.

I fidget in my seat. A small voice in the back of my mind whispers about the differences in our lives. It reminds me how different it is here compared to where I started life in San Francisco. I glance at Megan and tell the voice to fuck off.

My past doesn't define who I am. The here and now does.

Gramps whistles low. "What, you got a pool and all?"

"Hope you brought your swimming trunks," she comments in a chipper voice.

"Good job I did, then." Gramps pats his stomach. "Love a good swim."

She turns the car onto a driveway leading to one of the three-story houses. The drive is lined by circular bushes and winter flowers. I look up at the house. Painted white, it looks like something out of a movie.

You know ... The ones where the rich, unattainable person always lives.

You're not worth anything. I clench my jaw and push the voice away. I won't let it ruin this weekend for Megan.

Megan hops out of the car. The front door opens, revealing a woman that could be Megan in twenty years' time. Looking at her mom's blonde hair, slender figure and bright smile, it's easy to see exactly why Megan is so damn beautiful.

Gramps whistles again. "That's one hot momma," he whispers to me, chuckling.

I roll my eyes and step from the car, turning to help him out. He waves me off, and I roll my eyes again. Damn stubborn man.

He brushes his hands off on his legs. "I'm going to meet me some beautiful ladies." He hobbles up the drive on his stick, approaching Megan and her mom, and promptly introduces himself. I smirk when he leans forward to kiss Megan's mom on the cheek, taking her totally by surprise. She laughs, and Megan turns to me, smiling.

My stomach jolts, and I repeat my mantra in my mind. My past does not define me. My past does not define me.

"Mom, this is Aston. Aston, this is my mom, Gloria," Megan introduces us.

"It's lovely to meet you, Aston." Gloria's eyes twinkle with genuine happiness. She holds her hand out, and I take it, kissing her fingers.

"The pleasure is all mine."

She beams, leaning into Megan. "And he's polite! I like him already."

Gramps winks at me, and I stifle my grin as Gloria

leads us into the house. Megan slips her hand inside mine, and I squeeze it lightly.

"Roger?" Gloria calls. "Where are you?"

"In the yard, darling," a deep voice calls back.

"He's getting the grill fired up," she explains, leading us into the house.

It looks nothing like I expected it to. In my mind it was immaculate and filled with expensive trinkets, but it's not. The walls are adorned with certificates with Megan's name on – from swimming to horse riding, pictures of her and Braden and family photos. My eyes flick from one image to another, drinking them in.

"You were a really cute kid," I murmur as we pass a photo of Megan with her hair in pigtails, grinning at the camera with a tooth missing.

"Shut up," she mutters back. I grin.

The back yard is about the size of Gramps' house. He whistles again, and I resist the urge to join him. We step onto the decking that houses the grill, a large table and chairs, and a few random plants. A pool house is at the far end next to a fair sized pool.

And you could still get another house in the free space.

I knew Braden and Megan came from money, but holy fucking shit.

"Megs!" The man at the grill calls, turning around.

"Dad," Megan groans, and I see why. His apron is that of a naked guy's – sporting a six pack and burger bun over the space where his privates should be. I chuckle.

"What?" he says innocently.

"You had to wear that apron, didn't you? Remember? Guests?" she implores desperately.

He looks at me and Gramps. "Too late now, darling daughter. They've already seen it!"

"And I've got a real one!" Gramps laughs throatily, patting his rounded stomach. He steps forward and introduces himself to Megan's dad.

Megan sighs and rests her forehead against my shoulder. I kiss the top of her head.

"And this must be the boy that stole my girl's heart." Her dad turns to me, smiling widely.

"Yes, sir." I wink at Megan. She's giving her dad the death stare.

"Roger," he introduces himself, shaking my free hand. "Sure is nice to meet you, Son. If she ever had a boyfriend in high school, we never got to meet him. Braden scared him off before we even got close."

"*Dad!*" Megan gasps. "What are you talking about?"

"The fact you never brought me some eye candy home from school," a smoky voice rasps from the kitchen. "About time you did. He has a nice behind. Is his front that nice?"

"Mother," Gloria warns.

I raise an eyebrow at Megan, and her mouth drops open. A slight flush rises on her cheeks, and we both turn to look at the old woman sweeping out of the house onto the decking.

"What? I was talking about the fine gentleman sitting

at the table over here." She takes a seat opposite Gramps and runs her eyes across me. "Although, good choice, Megan. He's a pretty one."

"And he has brains." Megan shrugs.

"Go off to college and you get picky. Mind you …" Her nan grins. "I'd be picky too, if he was on offer."

"And he got them looks and brains from somewhere," Gramps butts in.

"And it was clearly you." Her nan beams at him. They strike up a conversation, and I smile. Bringing him here was a good idea.

"So you really never had a boyfriend in high school?" I tease Megan.

She opens her mouth, closes it, and opens it again.

"Not one she brought home," Gloria explains. "Braden definitely scared them off, so imagine my shock when she told me about you! I thought you were definitely going to show up with a broken arm or a black eye."

"A broken arm?" Roger exclaims, poking the coal. "I expected him to show up in a wheelchair. Maybe that girl is good for Braden."

"Maddie," Megan corrects. "Not 'that girl', Dad. Her name is Maddie."

"That's it. I knew it was an 'M' name, I just couldn't think of it." He waves her off.

"Perhaps." Gloria smiles. "Megan, why don't you go and show Aston around? It looks as though his grandfather is occupied for the moment." She leans forward. "I made the spare rooms up because I didn't know what you were doing," she whispers. "If you want to share, you go ahead. You're adults, after all, but just use–"

"Yes, thank you, Mom," Megan rushes out. "Understood."

She tugs on my hand, pulling me away from the decking and her father's laughter. I smirk to myself.

"Good grief," she says when we're inside. "That went kinda well, I guess."

"Hey – your parents embarrassed you, and your Nan eyed me up. I'd say it went pretty well!"

She pauses. "I guess that's kinda standard."

"I dunno. I've never met the parents before."

She pauses halfway up the stairs, tilting her head and looking at me. "Really?"

"Yeah. You sound surprised."

"I kinda am."

"Why? You know I've never really dated anyone before. It's always just been casual."

She starts walking again. "So … This is serious?" I catch the teasing lilt in her voice.

"I'm toying with the idea of it …"

She grins, and I pull her close at the top of the stairs. "Yes?" She bats her eyelashes as she looks up at me.

I smile. "Was there ever any doubt this was serious?"

"No," she answers, kissing me. "Not really."

"Not really?" I raise an eyebrow.

"No," she corrects, pulling me toward a door. "Love you."

Her words send warmth through my body, silencing

the constant whisper in the back of my mind.

"Love you," I whisper, kissing her nose.

"My room." She opens the door behind her, and I follow her in.

Woah.

Stuffed toys sit on the dresser, the white rug on the floor is fluffy as hell, and the walls are painted a light purple. Two doors to the right lead to what I assume is an en-suite and walk-in closet, and fairy lights hang above her bed.

"I'm pretty sure this is the most girly room I've ever seen in my life."

"And how many girls' rooms have you seen, exactly?" She quirks her eyebrows.

"One. This one."

"Then your statement is ridiculous." She laughs.

"I'm sleeping in here?" I eye up the stuffed toys.

"You don't have to."

"I'm not saying I don't want to. I do." I point to the stuffed toys. "But they're gonna have to be turned around. I'm really not into being perved on by damn stuffed bears."

Her blue eyes twinkle and she rests against the wall. "There's nothing wrong with my stuffed bears."

"There's nothing right with them, baby."

"Are you making me choose between you and my bears?"

"Yes. Yes, I am."

"I can see this being an issue, Mr. Banks."

"Is that so, Miss Harper?" I step toward her, pulling

her to me. My fingers thread through her hair, tilting her head back, and I brush my lips across hers. "Can your stuffed bears do this?" I run my nose along her jaw, my lips peppering kisses down her neck, sucking lightly on her pulse point. Her breath catches. "Or this?" I slide my hand down her back to cup her ass and pull her hips against mine. My erection throbs lightly against her, growing as she grinds slightly. "Or this?" I bend my head and swirl my tongue across the swell of her breasts, teasing her by dipping it along the cup of her bra.

"No," she breathes out. "No. They can't do that."

I nibble my way up to her ear, resting my lips against it. "So what was the issue?" I whisper.

"Issue? Who said anything about an issue?" She puts her fingers in my hair and tugs my head back. "No issues here."

My lips twitch. "So the bears get turned round?"

She nods. "Hell, if there's more of that …" Her body pushes right against mine, aligning perfectly. "They can live in the pool for all I care."

"Oh, there's plenty more where that came from, and it's all yours."

~

Megan runs her hand down my body, her fingers tracing the defining lines of the muscle. I sigh deeply, pulling her closer to me, and breathe in the vanilla scent of her hair. No matter where she's been or what she's done, she always smells like vanilla.

"What are we doing today?" I ask, my fingertips following the curve of her spine right to her ass.

She shudders. "I thought we could go riding."

"I get the feeling we're not talking about bedroom riding."

She looks up at me, her hair messy, and smiles. "No. Horse riding. I don't go at college and I miss it."

"I've never ridden a horse."

"I'll teach you."

"Um."

"You taught me to fish," she reminds me. "You made me fish!"

"I guess there's no way around this, huh?"

She shakes her head, rolling on top of me. Her knees go either side of my hips, trapping me, and her hair falls around my face. She slowly lowers her face to mine, sucking my bottom lip into her mouth and grazing her teeth across it. I slide my hands along her thighs, my thumbs coming dangerously close to the naked area of warmth between her legs.

"No way around it at all," she whispers.

"Really? You can't ride me instead?"

"I . . ." she stops as I flick my thumb across her clit gently, making her thighs tighten. "I'm sure."

She grabs my hands and moves them away.

"Is it gonna be one of those days?" I sigh.

She goes to her dresser, and slides on a pair of white lace panties and matching bra. My eyes follow her every movement as she walks into her closet soundlessly. I sit up and reaching forward to grab some clean boxers from my bag. Reaching forward very fucking uncomfortably thanks to the hardness of my dick. I shove them on as Megan reappears wearing riding pants and a white shirt.

"Fuck."

She might as well be naked the way those pants cling to her hips. They're molded to her body like a second skin.

"I have to watch you ride a horse wearing those pants?" I clarify, half hoping she'll be putting a baggier pair over them.

She ties her hair into a messy bun on top of her head and turns to me, her pink lips curved in a smile. "Yep."

I stand up and pull my own pants on. "Please tell me it's easy to ride a horse with a hard on."

She covers her mouth with her hand and lets out a loud laugh, her eyes flicking to my dick. "I've never, um, tried it. Not personally."

I pull my shirt on. "This is gonna be a fuckin' nightmare."

"But I'd imagine it's pretty hard."

"Yeah? Then at least I have something in common with it."

~

Megan pulls up outside a row of old stables on the edge of Palm Springs. There's nothing beyond them except open space, and I can see why the stables were built here.

"This is the place I learned to ride. I called ahead this morning and asked them to saddle the horses up for us." She smiles at me.

"Right." I look dubiously at the stables.

"Come on!" She gets out of the car, and I follow suit. "Oh, and, um, don't go caveman, okay?"

"Why would I go caveman?"

"The owner's son may have a teeny tiny crush on me."

I look at her blankly.

"He's only just sixteen," she carries on. "He's crushed on me since he could walk."

"Right." I have to ride with a boner and deal with a sixteen year old guy making eyes at my girl. Who said this was a good idea?

"Oh, Aston." She laughs, grabbing my hands. "Don't be grumpy. He's cute."

"Cute?"

"As in sweet-cute, not hot-cute."

"Am I cute?"

"You're hot-cute." She tugs me forward and kisses my cheek. "There is a big, big difference."

I grin as she leads me over to a stable with two brown horses. Her smile widens and she drops my hand, racing over to one of them. She runs her hand down the horse's nose and hugs its neck.

"Hello, boy," she coos. "Did you miss me?" She nuzzles her face into the horse's neck, and I find myself smiling. That is definitely sweet-cute.

I keep my distance. I'm really not a horse guy. I have no idea why I'm here.

Megan turns to me, a light in her eyes and a huge smile on her face.

Scratch that shit. I know exactly why I'm here. I'm here because this makes her happy, and if I wanna do anything in my life, it's make this girl happy. No matter what it takes or whatever I have to do to achieve it, I'll do my damnedest to put that smile on her face as many times as I can.

She unbolts the door and leads the horse out, patting his neck. "This is Storm. He's my baby." She glances at me. "He was my sweet sixteenth present. Most people got a car. I got a horse, and worked for my Dad for a year to get my car."

"Isn't a horse cheaper?"

"It depends, but my boy is a thoroughbred and worth more than I could have earned in the year leading up to my birthday. Besides, a car is a car. Storm is one of my favorite guys."

"I thought I heard your voice," a woman calls and appears from the back of the stable. "It's good to see you, Megs. Your boy has missed you." The woman pats Storm.

"I missed him." Megan smiles at her. "June, this is Aston, my boyfriend. Aston, this is June. She owns the stables and takes care of Storm for me while I'm at college."

"It's nice to meet you," I say.

"So you're the reason she called ahead? Learning to

ride?"

"Yes, ma'am."

She nods approvingly. "Nice choice, Megan. He's cute."

Megan snorts into her hand. "I'm getting that a lot."

"I don't mind." I grin.

"Let's just hope Poppy thinks you're cute. She likes beginners, and if you chuck her one of these . . ." She throws me an apple I didn't even realize she was holding. ". . . She'll love you forever."

"Where is she, then? I'll go charm her." I wink at Megan, and throw and catch the apple.

"This is Poppy." June unlocks a door and leads out a white horse with gray speckles. "She's the calmest of the bunch and she's been with me for six years. She'll take care of you."

I walk up to her, gently reaching out to rub her neck and offering the apple. She takes it, eating it in under a minute, and nudges my shoulder with her nose.

"You're not having any more," June scolds her. "You be nice to Aston, old girl. Megan likes him."

Megan reaches over and pats her nose. "Hey, girl. Ready to ride?"

Poppy neighs in what I assume is a yes, and both women lead the horses to the paddock. I follow behind, lagging slightly. Horse-riding. I never thought I'd see the day I'd be riding a horse – especially not to make a girl happy. I shake my head in a mild sort of amusement.

"Right." June waves me over to her, and I watch

Megan expertly mount Storm. Those pants are tight as fuck. Crap.

"Yep." I stand next to Poppy, staring at the saddle.

"Gather the reins in one hand, put your left foot in the stirrup, and hold onto the wither," June orders me. "Then push up and swing your leg over her flank. Make sure you don't kick her."

"What if I do?"

"Then she'll take off, and you'll land on your ass."

Megan giggles, and I shoot her a look. "No kicking horse ass. Got it."

"Ready? Go."

I do as she says, sitting on Poppy's saddle.

"Not bad," June praises. "Now let your legs hang down, and I'll sort out your stirrups."

She fiddles with them and instructs me on how to settle my feet in properly. She puts a hat on my head, tightens the strap under my chin, and pats Poppy's behind. She begins to move and I grab the reins tighter.

"Holy–"

"Sit up straight!" June barks. "Megan, he's all yours!"

"Thanks, June!" She waves her off, and Poppy follows Storm out into the paddock. Megan turns to me, grinning. "Whatever you do, don't squeeze your legs."

"Why not?" I mutter, wishing I could lean forward and grab the horse's neck. I admit it. I'm scared of this damn beast.

"Because she'll go faster."

"Great. You couldn't have given me a run down on

the way here?"

"Did you tell me about fishing before we got on the boat?" Her eyes sparkle, and I nod my head toward her.

"Touché, baby. Touché."

She clicks her tongue, and Storm begins to move faster.

"I hope you're not expecting me to go any faster."

"I'm not," she calls. "I didn't actually expect you to get on Poppy!"

"Nice to know you have confidence in me," I shout dryly as she rounds behind me. Poppy's walking at a nice pace. I'm really not into taking her up into a trot. No way.

The ground is dusty as we leave the small paddock, and the sun beats down with a still hot temperature. "Where are we going?" I ask her.

"You'll see."

Chapter Twenty-Five - Megan

I slide down from Storm's back and pat his neck lovingly, hooking his reins around a tree branch in the shade. I take my helmet off, shake out my hair, and look under the roots for the basket I asked June to place there earlier. Storm turns his attention to the water I've given him, and I lie the blanket out on the ground on the other side of the small tree. Excited, I sit down and wait for Aston to catch up.

Palm Canyon trail is one of my favorite to take – it always has been. Sitting here by the stream and letting Storm rest was a weekly pastime before I left for Berkeley. We'd do the other trails on our other rides, but our Saturdays were always reserved for this.

And now I remember why.

The green of the fauna is a stark contrast to the barren desert beyond, and the rocks that dot the stream are just big enough to sit on. It's beautiful here. Peaceful in the winter when no one comes here.

"How do I get down?" Aston approaches.

I laugh at the sight of him. "Click your tongue three times, and she'll stop, then get down the way you got up."

"Not kicking her ass, right?"

"Exactly."

He clicks his tongue and Poppy stops. His dismount is swift and it looks like he could have been riding his whole life.

"A picnic?" he smirks, hooking her reins over the branch the way I did and removing his hat.

"Surprised?" I smile as he drops onto the blanket next to me.

"Yep, but then you always surprise me." He presses his lips to mine, and I cup the side of his face.

"You said you wanted to see Palm Springs. There's not much in the other direction you can't see in any other town, but this is my favorite place in the whole world." I drop my hand and look around. "I've missed it here. I didn't realize it until I was sitting here."

"It's pretty damn nice," Aston says appreciating the view. "You really grew up here?"

"Pretty much. My mom has her horse at the stables, too. You didn't see him, but Midnight is–"

"Black?"

"Yep, actually." I glance at him. "She grew up here and taught me to ride. We spent every weekend out here until I was fourteen and she let me come alone. I didn't miss a weekend until I started college."

"Did you not think about riding in Berkeley?"

I shake my head. "I don't think I have the time. Besides – I can't expect my parents to pay for it as well as college. I could get a job, but then I definitely wouldn't have time to ride. It's a lose-lose situation." I shrug.

Aston rummages in the basket. "At least you can still ride when you get home … Even if it is only a few times a year."

"True." I smile as he pulls out the strawberries. He grabs one from the dish and brings it close to my mouth. I hold it in place, and take a huge bite. Juice dribbles down my chin and he grins, flicking it away with his thumb.

"I hope you don't think I'm feeding you," he mutters, biting into his own strawberry.

"But you just did." I pout, looking at the other strawberry in his hand. "And that's a huge one!"

He looks at it, then at me and sighs. "Fine. Have the huge strawberry." He holds it out to me, and I lean forward, biting into it slowly, my lips wrapping around it. His eyes flick down, focusing on my mouth, and I sit back.

My lips curve up as he puts a hand just behind my back, his face coming close to mine.

"You have a little . . ." he whispers in a rough voice, bringing his thumb to my face. I glance down at it, watching as he presses it against the corner of my mouth softly, wiping along the curve of my bottom lip. I part my lips, drawing in a slow breath, and close my eyes as he sweeps his hand into my hair.

His breath is hot across my lips, mingling with mine, and my heart pounds as he hovers there above me, millimeters from touching me. It's a moment that seems to last forever, a moment filled with hope, anticipation, resolve, and *love*.

Hope for us. Anticipation for the future. Resolve to make it last. Love for everything we have and have yet to share together, and for everything we are.

And when he finally touches his lips to mine, it

makes it all the sweeter.

~

The ride back to the stables is easy – mostly because Aston realizes he isn't going to fall off if he goes into a trot. I let him drive back to my house and that seems to make up for forcing him to sit on a horse and stare at my ass in tight riding pants all day.

It kinda makes up for it, anyway.

Everyone is out when we arrive back, and I bet Mom dragged them all to the store. Tonight is her annual Thanksgiving eve party, which translates as lots of people, lots of wine, and lots of Nan eyeing up all the younger guys.

"You were a bit of an overachiever as a kid," Aston says as we go upstairs.

"I was?"

"Yep. Swimming, horse-riding, gymnastics … Anything else?"

"Hmm. I danced for a bit. Well, six months. I gave it up. I was too heavy on my feet from gym, and I was a terrible ballerina." I grin. "Gymnastics is a lot like dance, but apparently dance isn't a lot like gymnastics." I shrug, walking into my bathroom and running the shower.

I toss my clothes into the laundry basket and step under the steaming hot water, letting it run over me and soothe my aches from the day of riding. My legs are stiff and I know they'll be even worse tomorrow, but it was so worth it.

It was even more worth it because Aston got to know some of me after showing me so much of him. His life is stuck in San Francisco, and while my life is in Berkeley, my heart is in Palm Springs.

He needs a little shove to let his heart break completely free from the confines he keeps it in. He might have let it go a little for me, but he needs to let it go for himself.

I just hope this weekend can do that for him, even just a bit.

I begin to hum to myself as I wrap a towel around my body, the soft melody of *Cry With You* by Hunter Hayes filling the small room. I scan the rows of bottles and tubs on my shelves, grabbing a vanilla moisturizer to match my shampoo.

The unsung words of the song haunt me, resonating through my body as I perch my foot on the edge of the bathtub and rub the moisturizer along my leg. The song reminds me of Aston, all his pain and all the pain I feel for him. It reminds me how I know I'll never leave him, how I can give him the kind of love he needs to get through whatever his past throws at him.

Just like Hunter Hayes, I feel all the pain.

I let the towel fall away as I rub the moisturizer all over my body, letting it dry the water remaining on my skin. Two rough, warm hands cup my hips and a hot, chiseled chest presses against my back. Aston's lips blaze a trail across my shoulders, his hands moving to my stomach and holding me flat against him.

"Were you watching me?" My voice is slightly shaky.

"Would you slap me if I say yes?" he replies in my ear, his hands moving up to cup my breasts.

"No," I breathe out, pushing into his hands.

"Then yes, I was." He kisses my neck, his hands massaging me in a way that tugs on all my stomach muscles and starts a desperate ache between my legs.

"Why?"

"Because," he whispers. "I couldn't not. I don't know if you realize how beautiful you are with no make-up on, your wet hair, wearing just a tiny towel or nothing at all. I've never seen you totally natural before, and I didn't think you could be any more beautiful than you usually are, but you are."

He slides his hand down my stomach, easing his fingers between my thighs. He rubs his finger against my clit and pushes his hips into me, his erection digging in between my ass cheeks. My head drops back against him, and he blazes more kisses down my exposed neck, curving his fingers and soothing my ache. He keeps it up, holding me against him even as heat swamps my body and my legs give out. He holds me as the shaking subsides, still kissing me tenderly.

"My turn," I whisper, spinning in his arms. I cup him with my hand, running my fingers along the outside of his boxers. He tugs us back into my bedroom, and I creep my fingers inside his boxers to touch him fully. He's rock hard, and my fingers barely go right around him as they start a steady, pumping rhythm up and down him.

Aston pushes us onto the bed, moving his hips in time with my hand, and plunges his tongue into my mouth. The ache starts between my legs again, and I involuntarily buck my hips when he groans my name into my mouth. I squeeze him in my hand, not stopping my body's responses to the desperate exploration his hands are undertaking.

It doesn't take long before he pulls away from me, rolls on a condom and positions himself against me. He looks into my eyes as he pushes inside me, my muscles clenching around him. There are so many words I could say to him in this moment, so many things that need to be said between us, but this feels like it's meant to be.

The first time since we came out. The first time since we used the word love.

After, we both shower and get ready for Mom's party. My dress swishes about my knees as I stand and check my reflection in the mirror, smoothing the skirt out. Aston steps up behind me, linking his fingers with mine, and smiles.

"We make a pretty hot couple." He winks, and I laugh.

"I'm not used to having to share looks and brains with someone. I always assumed I'd be the smart one out of us," I tease him.

"Oh, you're the smart one, all right." He touches his lips to my temple. "You've taught me a lot in the last month. A lot I wouldn't have learned without you."

I reach up and touch his face, meeting his eyes in the mirror. "You don't know that."

"No, I do. When we were on the trail today and we stopped for lunch, you taught me how something barren and empty can be full of life and beautiful."

My lips twist up slightly. "The canyon was deserted," I remind him.

"But it was full of life because of you," he says honestly. "You added to the beauty of it, bringing a desolate place alive. Just like you did for me. I always thought I was dead inside, that I had to feel that way. That I couldn't remember because remembering meant feeling, and feeling meant being. And then there was you. You made me remember what it was like to live."

"Aston . . ." I take a deep breath. "But none of that matters if it's all for me. You have to ask yourself who you live for."

"At first it was you. All you. Now? Now it's a little of both. You taught me how to love, and I'm pretty sure I love myself just a little bit, now. I'll never see what you see, but it's more than I've ever had."

I blink harshly, trying not to cry, because he can't possibly understand how much those words mean to me. He can't understand how much I wanted to make that pain better for him, make him understand he's more than he thought. And he definitely can't understand how his words seal around my heart, gripping onto it like a vice.

"Really?" I whisper.

'Her heart did whisper that he had done it for her.'

"Really, baby. I live for me, but I love for you." He kisses my temple again, and I feel every word.

He was always my Mr. Darcy.

And I was always his Elizabeth.

Epilogue – Aston

I tug the zipper of my jacket up higher as a cold wind blows in off San Francisco Bay, and fight the urge to turn and run back to the marina. I won't run. This is something that has to be done, for me.

Megan squeezes my hand, curling into my arm, and we begin to walk into the small cemetery where my mom lies.

I feel sick. Emotion stronger than I've felt in a long time swirls around my whole body, from hatred to pity, fear to anger, yet through it all … Through it all is a bit of love for the woman that tried and failed to give me life.

We weave silently through the graves and markers, heading to the back of the cemetery. I hold the white rose I bought tightly, clutching it to my chest, and try to breathe deeply.

I will never forgive her and I will never forget her, but I can finally be at peace with her.

The small, black marble headstone sits alongside my Gran's, and Megan places a small bunch of flowers against it silently. My eyes trace the letters of Mom's gravestone, following the engraved patterns, and it begins to blur as my eyes sting with tears.

I sink down to my knees in front of the stone, letting the tears fall as they need to, and set the rose down. The white of the rose is a stark contrast to the black of the marble, like my childhood innocence was a contrast to my mom's mature promiscuity.

Even now, it follows her. In life and in death.

"We're at peace now, Mom," I say softly into the wind. "Whatever it was that made you the way you were, I'm glad you're away from it. I'm sorry I wasn't enough for you. Maybe I was too much. I'll never know. I just hope you're at peace now. And I . . . I love you."

There are so many more words. I could yell at her grave, scream at it if I really wanted, but it won't have any effect on it. She'll still be gone and it won't change anything. Hating her can't change the past, and I finally know that. Hating her won't make it all go away. It won't erase it.

I stand and look into Megan's clear blue eyes. She clasps my hand, holding on tightly, and I follow her from the cemetery. I said I'd never come back to San Francisco. I always knew I'd have to come back, and now I have. Now I don't ever have to come back. I don't have to look back. I can travel back across the water to college, and stay on that side of the water.

I can look into the blue eyes of the girl I love every day, and make the life I always wanted.

ABOUT EMMA HART:

By day, New York Times and USA Today bestselling New Adult author Emma Hart dons a cape and calls herself Super Mum to two beautiful babies.

Emma is working on Top Secret projects she will share with her followers and fans at every available opportunity. Naturally, all Top Secret projects involve a dashingly hot guy who likes to forget to wear a shirt, a sprinkling (or several) of hold-onto-your-panties hot scenes, and a whole lotta love.

She likes to be busy - unless busy involves doing the dishes, but that seems to be when all the ideas come to life.

Website: www. emmahart.org
Facebook: www.facebook.com/EmmaHartBooks
Twitter: https://twitter.com/EmmaHartAuthor
Email: emmaevelynx3@gmail.com
Goodreads:
http://www.goodreads.com/author/show/6451162.Emma_Hart

42913978R00162

Made in the USA
Lexington, KY
11 July 2015